## JESSI AND THE TROUBLEMAKER

Danielle was lying sprawled on the floor of the study with a small bookcase tipped over beside her and books all over the floor.

"Danielle!" I cried. "Are you all right?"

Sitting up, Danielle said, "Ooops!"

"Don't move," I said, visions of broken bones dancing in my head. "Does it hurt anywhere?"

"No," said Danielle, giving me a funny look. I suddenly realized that I might be overreacting just a little.

"Nothing hurts?" I said, just to be sure.

"No," replied Danielle.

I started to help her to her feet—and then I saw the Rollerblades.

# JESSI AND THE
# TROUBLEMAKER

## Ann M. Martin

*The author gratefully acknowledges
Nola Thacker
for her help in
preparing this manuscript.*

Scholastic Children's Books,
Commonwealth House, 1–19 New Oxford Street, London,
WC1A 1NU, UK
a division of Scholastic Ltd
London ~ New York ~ Toronto ~ Sydney ~ Auckland

First published in the US by Scholastic Inc., 1995
First published in the UK by Scholastic Ltd, 1997

Text copyright © Ann M. Martin, 1995
THE BABYSITTERS CLUB is a registered trademark of
Scholastic Inc.

ISBN 0 590 19260 4

All rights reserved

Typeset by Rowland Phototypesetting Ltd,
Bury St Edmunds, Suffolk
Printed by Cox & Wyman Ltd, Reading, Berks.

10 9 8 7 6 5 4 3 2 1

The right of Ann M. Martin to be identified as the
author of this work has been asserted by her in accordance
with the Copyright, Designs and Patents Act, 1988.

This book is sold subject to the condition that it shall not, by
way of trade or otherwise, be lent, resold, hired out, or otherwise
circulated without the publisher's prior consent in any form of
binding or cover other than that in which it is published and
without a similar condition, including this condition, being
imposed upon the subsequent purchaser.

# 1st
# CHAPTER

"I like the snow," I said.

Mallory Pike, who was walking beside me, didn't answer. She rubbed one mittened hand across the front of her glasses.

"I mean, it's *so* beautiful. And think of all the great ballets with snow in them."

"I wish my glasses had little windscreen wipers," answered Mallory. "*Then* I might agree with you." She paused. "What ballets?"

"Oh . . . well, *The Nutcracker*, for one." I did a sort of pirouette on the pavement—and slipped.

"Hey," said Mallory, catching my arm. We laughed. Then she added, "It *is* pretty. I just wish it would stick."

"I don't think it's cold enough," I said with regret.

"Well, I'm officially complaining here.

If it is going to be winter, it should act like winter. It should snow *and* stick."

In case you've just pirouetted into the middle of all this (if you know what I mean), I should explain.

I'm Jessi. Jessi Ramsey. I'm in sixth grade at Stoneybrook Middle School, also known as SMS, in Stoneybrook, Connecticut. Mallory Pike is my best friend, and also a fellow member of the Baby-sitters Club (also known as the BSC and more about that later). Being in SMS together and being members of the BSC are just two of the things that Mallory and I share. Walking home from school, and horse stories, especially stories by Marguerite Henry, are some of the other things we have in common, which is part of the reason we are best friends.

Liking snow and wishing for a real snowstorm might be counted in the things we have in common, too.

But not dancing. In case you hadn't guessed, I want to be a ballet dancer one day. I have special lessons and I get up every morning at 5:29 A.M. to practise. My family's even arranged a practice area in the basement for me, and they drive me up and down to Stamford to study at the Stamford Ballet School.

Mallory, on the other hand, hates anything athletic except maybe archery. She wants to be a children's book writer and illustrator. Maybe, I tell her, one day she'll write a book about a ballet dancer and use me as the model for the illustrations. Maybe, she tells me, one day I'll be so famous that I won't be the model—maybe the whole book will be about me. And then we'll both be famous.

That would be cool.

But meanwhile, walking home with Mallory (and finishing another day of school) was pretty excellently cool, too.

"Do you want to come in?" I asked when we reached my house. "See if we can make some hot chocolate?"

Mallory shook her head and wiped her mitten across her glasses again. "I wish I could, but I have to get home. Mum's taking Byron, Adam and Jordan to the dentist this afternoon. I'm going to keep an eye on things while she's gone."

Keeping an eye on things was putting it mildly. That's another way Mallory and I are different: I come from a fairly standard sized family and she comes from a *huge* one. She has seven brothers and sisters, and three of her brothers—the ones who were going to the dentist—are identical triplets. Having helped Mal babysit for all her brothers and sisters, I know what chaos it can be.

I know it gets to Mal, too, sometimes. But it also makes her an incredibly calm babysitter. Between them, her four brothers have thought up just about every way of getting into trouble, intentionally or not, that seems possible. Hardly anything rattles Mallory now, at least in the babysitting department.

"I'll call you later," added Mallory. She waved goodbye and set off for home.

I hurried up the drive (but no pirouetting!) and into the kitchen. "I'm home!" I called out.

A massive rattling and clanging met my ears, like a doorbell gone beserk. Or a couple of empty dustbins doing a dustbin dance.

Sure enough, my baby brother Squirt was sitting on the kitchen floor, banging on an assortment of pots and pans with a metal spoon and various lids. He was wearing a saucepan on his head.

I burst out laughing. "Mr John Philip Ramsey, Junior, you are super cute," I said.

Squirt didn't understand all I was saying, but he knew it was good. He smiled a baby-toothed smile at me, which made him look even cuter, and dropped a lid into a frying pan.

"La la la la BANG!" he said.

Aunt Cecelia looked up from the kitchen worktop, where she had opened a book.

"What're you doing?" I asked. "Are you cooking something special? Are you making dinner tonight?"

"I'm thinking," she said.

"What about?"

Aunt Cecelia made a note on a piece of paper on the worktop next to her and said, "You'll see soon enough. You aren't walking snow and mud into the house, are you? Take your shoes off."

I hid a smile. That was just like Aunt Cecelia. When she'd first moved in with us to help look after us after my mum went back to work full-time in advertising (my father already had a full-time job outside the house, but Mama had stopped when I was born), I'd had a real problem with her. I thought she was far too strict and old-fashioned. But I've got used to her ways and she's got used to mine, and mostly we get along pretty well now.

And Squirt *loves* her.

I took my shoes off and put them by the kitchen door. I hung my coat on the coat rack on the wall above the shoes. Just then, my eight-year-old sister Becca wandered into the kitchen.

"Hi, Jessi," she said.

Squirt did something really loud and creative with his pots-and-pans drum set and Becca covered her ears. "That's nice, Squirt!" she practically shouted.

"Enough nice," said Aunt Cecelia. She bent and scooped Squirt up and pretended to hold him upside down. Squirt shrieked happily.

Becca and I knew what to do. We scooped up Squirt's pots and pans and put them out of sight. When Aunt Cecelia put him back down, he looked around for a moment, sort of puzzled, then set off at a high-speed crawl across the floor towards the door leading to the hall.

Aunt Cecelia wrote something else down on the piece of paper, folded it up, and put it in her pocket. "I've got to go and do some errands for a little while, Jessi. So I'm going to leave you in charge, okay?"

"No problem," I said.

"Gogo," said Squirt. "Gogo!"

He wanted to be in his wheelie walker. It was a sort of baby-powered baby buggy. When you put Squirt in it, he could zoom around the house on his own without falling. Actually, Squirt (the nurses gave him that nickname when he was born because he was the smallest baby at the hospital, only five pounds, eight ounces) is growing pretty fast now and has learned to walk pretty well. He really doesn't need his baby walker. But he still loves it. We have to keep a close eye on him when he's zooming, though. He likes to zoom into things. He likes the noise it makes. Not surprising, is it?

A few minutes later, Aunt Cecelia was out of the door and Squirt was bumping up and down the hall (we'd closed all the doors so he couldn't make any sneak attacks on empty rooms when we weren't looking).

"I've been thinking of adding a couple of new things to my Kid-Kit," I told Becca. "Got any ideas?" (My sister's name is Rebecca, by the way. All three of the kids in my family have nicknames: I'm Jessica, obviously, and you know Squirt's real name, which he'll grow into, eventually.)

Becca's eyes lit up. Even though she's my sister and knows everything that goes into the Kid-Kit (as some of it is her old stuff) she still thinks it's special. Becca also likes helping people. She's even a member of an after-school club at Stoneybrook Elementary called the

Kids-Can-Do-Anything Club, or the Kids Club for short. As you might have guessed, it's a club for kids in which they think up ways to help in the community, such as collecting toys or writing letters to kids in hospital.

The Kid-Kit isn't a community activity, of course. It's a babysitting aid. Our BSC chairman, Kristy Thomas, thought of it (just one of her many brilliant but typically Kristy ideas, and more about her later, too). Everyone in the BSC has her own Kid-Kit, filled with games and toys and books and puzzles, new things that we buy out of our babysitting subs as well as some of our old things. We take the kits with us on babysitting jobs and the kids *love* them. They don't care if some of the books have already been read, or the puzzles have been used. To them, the stuff is new, because they've never seen it before. And have you ever noticed how kids really like to play with other kids' toys? Something about the grass being greener on the other side of the fence, maybe.

Anyway, it was time to add some new oomph to the old Kid-Kit. Mine is a little different from the others. It has a sort of "office" theme, which means that as well as a puzzle and one or two books (right now I have one about animals and animal jobs), the kit is filled with felt tips, pens, rubbers, coloured pencils, red, white, and blue paper clips, blunt scissors, tape, a memo pad, rubber bands, stickers, animal stamps, writing paper and envelopes.

"I'll go and get the Kid-Kit. I know where it is," said Becca and jumped up. She came back with the box and put it on the table. We opened it and looked inside.

"This puzzle has got to go," I said. It was a puzzle of the United States. "It's missing two pieces—two whole states."

Becca giggled. "Which ones?"

"Texas," I said. "And Kansas."

"Kansas is an easy one," said Becca. "That's a pity. It's square and it fits right in."

"I know."

"I've got a puzzle of a butterfly. I've done it lots and lots," Becca said. "Maybe you can put that in the Kid-Kit."

"That would be great!" I said. "What about a new book?"

"An office book?" asked Becca.

I nodded. "Or something about working." We both thought hard and then Becca said slowly, "I've got a book that I was saving for Squirt, but you could use it now for a little while."

"What is it?"

"*Bea and Mr Jones*," said Becca. "Amy Schwartz wrote it and drew the pictures."

"Great idea, Becca." And it was, too. *Bea and Mr Jones* is a picture book about a little girl who swaps places with her father. It's really funny and clever.

Becca went looking for the butterfly puzzle and the book. We were reading the book together (Squirt zoomed in and zoomed out again, intent on banging into as many things as possible) and laughing aloud when the doorbell rang.

I went to the door, stepping over Squirt, who was *still* zooming (although a little less energetically). Standing on the front door step were Charlotte Johanssen, Becca's best friend, and Danielle Roberts, another friend of theirs. Charlotte's not only Becca's best friend, but she's one of the kids the BSC members sit for. Danielle and her family weren't BSC clients at first, but I had got to know her through the Kids Club, when I volunteered to help once while one of the regular sponsors was away.

Hiding a smile, I said, "Who are you? What do you want?" Charlotte and Danielle giggled.

"Charlotte! Danielle!" Becca cried, coming out into the hall.

"Do you know these people?" I asked Becca and they all started to laugh.

I stepped back and invited them in, reminding them to take off their boots and hang up their coats (Aunt Cecelia would have been proud of me).

"Could we go down into your ballet room?" asked Charlotte before she'd even taken her coat off.

I was surprised. Charlotte is eight-going-on-nine. (If you ask her how old she is, she usually says "almost nine". Have you ever noticed how kids will do that? Even if they've just had a birthday they'll tell you they're "almost" the next year older.) She hates sports as much as Mallory does. Not that ballet is a sport, but it does involve physical activity.

"Of course," I said, surprised.

"Great," said Danielle, giving me her super-special Danielle smile. She finished taking off her boots.

Danielle took off her wool cap and stuffed it into the pocket of her coat, and Charlotte finished taking off her winter gear and hanging up her coat.

"Do you, er, want some company?" I asked.

A furious exchange of eye signals went on among Becca, Char and Danielle. Then Becca said, "No. I mean, if that's

11

okay with you. We'll be very careful."

"You do that," I said. "No ripping the *barre* out of the wall."

Just then Squirt zoomed past us and through the kitchen door.

"Squirt!" Becca and I said at the same time.

We dashed down the hall and into the kitchen just in time to see Squirt crash his walker into the kitchen cabinet. The cabinet door popped open and the pots and pans fell out.

For a moment, Squirt looked pleased. Then he started to cry.

"You lot go on," I said. "I think it's time Squirt had a little nap."

I lifted Squirt up and rested him on my hip, wiping the tears off his cheeks. "What's the matter, maestro?" I said. "Are you tired of your pots-and-pans band?"

"No," said Squirt (his new favourite word for everything). He made a whimpering sound, but he didn't really sound committed to it. Bouncing him gently on my hip, I carried him upstairs to his bedroom and put him down for a nap. I found his copy of *Goodnight Moon*, sat next to him, and began to read.

Squirt sniffled for a little while, but I kept one hand on his foot (except when I turned the pages) and sort of rocked him in time to the words. After a while, the sniffling stopped. And just as I finished the book for the second time, I heard a tiny little baby snore.

Okay, call me a doting sister. I stood by his cot and admired him for a while.

When I got back downstairs, Aunt Cecelia was coming through the kitchen door.

"Where is everybody?" she asked.

"Hi," I said. "Squirt's asleep, Becca is in the basement with Char and Danielle, and I'm about to go and do some homework."

"Good," said Aunt Cecelia. I grinned and went to my room to work on my maths problems.

By the time I'd finished and gone back downstairs to see what was going on, Mama and Daddy had both got home from work. Daddy was chopping carrots in the kitchen while Aunt Cecelia stirred something in a pot on the stove. Mama was sitting at the kitchen table with her feet up on a chair, reading aloud from a gardening catalogue.

"Roses in the middle of winter!" Aunt Cecelia shook her head.

Mama grinned. "You've just got to believe it, Cecelia. Listen to this one: 'A lovely old-fashioned rose with strong, sweet fragrance, this floribunda . . .' hi, darling, how was school?" Mama reached out and pulled me over to give me a kiss on the cheek.

"Fine," I said.

"Dinner in half an hour," said Daddy.

"Can I help?" I asked.

"Time those two downstairs were getting home for their own dinners," said Aunt Cecelia.

"I'll go and tell them," I said.

I went down to the basement. At the bottom of the stairs, I stopped.

Becca, Char and Danielle were sitting in front of the mirror by the *barre* writing furiously on pieces of paper. As I watched, Becca held up what she had written so that it was reflected in the mirror. Char and Danielle leaned forward and squinted. "B . . . billy," Char read aloud. "Billy Dobson is . . . etuc?"

"Etuc? What's etuc?" asked Danielle.

"Nooo! *Cute*," said Becca. The three girls fell backwards, shrieking and giggling.

"Now let's write it in mirror writing," said Char.

I cleared my throat.

Becca quickly covered up her piece of paper. "Hi, Jessi," she said.

"Practising ballet?" I asked.

"Er, resting," said Danielle quickly.

"It's time for you lot to go home. Almost dinner time."

They jumped up, gathering pieces of paper covered with all kinds of backward writing that was readable when held up to a mirror, and hurried upstairs.

"See you tomorrow," said Becca, waving goodbye at the door.

"Mirror, mirror on the wall, who's the cutest boy of all?" I teased Becca gently.

Becca ducked her head and looked at me out of the corner of her eye. Then a dimple appeared in her cheek. "Billy Dobson," she said and raced back up the hall to the kitchen.

"Don't run in the house," I heard Aunt Cecelia say.

Poking her head back out of the kitchen door, Becca said, "He's *etuc!*"

"Etuc yourself, Becca Ramsey," I said, grinning as I went to help my family finish getting ready for dinner. "Very etuc!"

# 2nd CHAPTER

The next day, you couldn't tell snow had ever fallen from the beautiful blue skies of Stoneybrook. Okay, so it was a little cold. But the sun was shining—and I got every maths problem right in my homework, which made it shine even brighter. Naturally, I was in a pretty good mood by the time I turned up for the BSC meeting at Claudia's house.

I was a little late because I'd just come from my dance class in Stamford. Claudia had left the front door unlocked (as usual) for the club members, and I pushed it open and hurried to her room.

From her throne (really, it's just a director's chair) Kristy Thomas, BSC chairman, idea-master, and strict time-keeper, gave me a Look as I walked into the room.

16

"Sorry," I said. "I've just got out of ballet class."

With a welcoming smile, Mallory scooted over and made room for me on the floor in front of Claudia's bed.

"Have a biscuit," said Claudia, who was sitting on her desk chair. "No, have two biscuits. Ballet dancers have to keep their strength up."

I grinned and took a chocolate-chip biscuit from the bag Claudia was holding out. "I thought we finished these at the last meeting."

"Two bags," explained Claudia.

Just then Stacey rushed into the room. I was surprised. I'm occasionally late (and used to getting Looks from Kristy) because of dance class, but Stacey is *never* late.

We all looked at her but she only said, "Sorry."

Claudia tossed Stacey a box of oatmeal raisin Frookies (biscuits made without sugar). Stacey fished one out and started nibbling on it without saying anything else.

Kristy gave Stacey a Look, too. Then she said, "Any new business?" letting us know that we *were* having a meeting, not a party.

Everyone looked around. Kristy took a

bite of the chocolate-chip biscuit in her hand and chewed ferociously.

No one said anything.

"Okay, no new business," said Kristy. We relaxed a little. The phone rang and Kristy answered it. "Babysitters Club."

How did Kristy know it was a client? I think I'd better explain how the BSC works. But I'd better begin at the beginning, right?

The beginning. When Kristy was in seventh grade, she was sitting at home one night listening to her mother trying to find a babysitter for her younger brother David Michael. As Mrs Thomas made phone call after phone call, Kristy had one of her brilliant ideas. What if a person could make just one phone call and reach several babysitters? That way, she'd be sure of getting a babysitter straight away, without all the hassle.

Before you could say *pas de deux* (that means dance for two, roughly), Kristy had enlisted her best friend Mary Anne Spier and another good friend, Claudia Kishi. Claudia invited Stacey McGill, a new friend of hers, to join, and the BSC was off and running.

Was it a brilliant idea? Well, it was so brilliant that in no time the four of them had more work than they could handle.

That's when Mary Anne and Dawn became friends and soon after, Dawn became part of the BSC.

Plenty of members, right? Wrong!

Mallory and I were the next to join, as junior officers. (We're both in sixth grade and everyone else is in eighth grade. Until we are older we can't babysit at night except for our own families, so we take care of a lot of the afternoon and week-end-day business.) And now the BSC has two associate members as well: Shannon Kilbourne and Logan Bruno.

We're all pretty different from one another. But as we like to point out, it's our differences that make us such a good club. We have a lot of different talents and skills among us—enough to handle any situation that comes up.

For example, there's Kristy. Kristy is our chairman not only because the club was her idea (along with some other great ideas I'll tell you about in a minute), but also because she is the Queen of the Organized People of Earth. She is chairman of the BSC, she coaches a kids' softball team called Kristy's Krushers, made up of kids of all ages, she does well at school, and she has a (sort-of) boyfriend, Bart, who coaches a rival softball team called Bart's Bashers.

Maybe being in a large family makes a person more organized (it's one of the theories I have about large families, but I never can remember to ask Mal if it's true). Like Mal, Kristy's from a large family, although hers is a very different mix. She lives in a mansion with two older brothers, Sam and Charlie; her younger brother, David Michael; her mother; her stepfather, Watson Brewer (Kristy's father left when she was just a kid and now she hardly ever hears from him); two step-siblings, Karen and Andrew, who stay there part of the time; Emily Michelle, who is adopted; Nannie, her maternal grandmother, who helps keep the house organized; one dog; one cat; two goldfish; a part-time hermit crab; a part-time rat; and a ghost.

Okay, maybe there isn't a ghost living in the mansion on the second floor, but you get the idea.

Kristy grew up with Mary Anne Spier, who is the BSC secretary. Mary Anne and Kristy are both different *and* alike. They're both short (Kristy is the shortest person in her class) and have brown hair, were brought up for part of their lives by single parents, now have "blended" families, and have always lived in Stoneybrook. In fact, they've known each other most of their lives. Kristy used to live next door to Mary Anne until her mum married Watson Brewer and her family moved into his house. Then Mary Anne's father remarried and she moved to a new house in Stoneybrook, too.

But while Kristy is like a living illustration of "the squeaky wheel gets the grease" (meaning it's the person who speaks up who gets what she wants), Mary Anne is just the opposite. Not that she's a wimp. But she is very shy and sensitive, someone who cries easily and has a tender heart. She is also stubborn and very strong. Mary Anne was brought up by her father (her mother died when Mary Anne was just a baby), who was very strict. Some kids would have wilted under all that loving strictness (Mr Spier just wanted to make sure, as a single parent, that he did everything *right*) but when Mary Anne realized she was outgrowing the little-girl clothes and the plaits he made her wear, she stood up for herself. Now she can dress the way she wants (within reason, which means that she just dresses casually, like Kristy, but a little more fashionably) and she can wear a little make-up. And she was even the first of us to have a steady boyfriend, Logan Bruno.

Mary Anne's life has changed a lot recently, and not just because she and her father have worked out a less strict, less formal relationship. One of the big changes is that her father got remarried — to Dawn Schafer's mum! They were high school sweethearts right here in Stoneybrook, but after graduation they went their separate ways. When Dawn's mum returned with her family to Stoneybrook from California after getting divorced, they got back together again, with a little help from Mary Anne and Dawn. Now they all live in an old farmhouse near the edge of town, except for Dawn's brother Jeff, who decided that he wanted to stay in California with his father. And Dawn and Mary Anne are best friends (yes, Mary Anne has two best friends).

As you might have guessed, Dawn, our alternate officer, (responsible for filling in when one of the other officers isn't there) is from California. And she misses it. She misses it so much that she's just spent a huge chunk of time there with her father and Jeff. But now she's back, and everyone is very glad.

Dawn looks like an advertisement for the benefits of exercise and healthy eating. It sounds corny, but it's true. She's really beautiful, with long, pale blonde hair, blue eyes, and a strong, tall body (she's got the perfect body to be a ballet dancer!). Dawn never, ever eats red meat and she hardly ever eats sweets. She's environmentally conscious (she carries a string bag with her wherever she goes so she doesn't have to use plastic, brings her lunch to school wrapped in greaseproof paper or reusable containers, and rides her bike whenever she can). And Dawn is as stubborn as, well, Kristy and Mary Anne. But she's also very mellow. Nothing seems to rattle Dawn, and she keeps a level head about almost everything— *very* important for a babysitter!

Another pair of best friends in the BSC is Stacey McGill and Claudia Kishi.

Stacey, who is a maths whiz, is the club treasurer. She's probably the most sophisticated of all of us. That's partly because Stacey has diabetes. That means her body doesn't regulate the amount of sugar in her blood, so she has to be really careful about what she eats. She can't eat sweets and she has to give herself injections of insulin every day. Because of that, Stacey's parents used to be really overprotective of her (sort of like Mary Anne's father; Stacey's also an only child, like Mary Anne) and Stacey had to convince them that she could be responsible about looking after herself. If she didn't, she could get really ill and even go into a coma.

Now Stacey has a bi-state family. (We tease Dawn about having a bi-coastal family, a family on each coast.) Stacey's mother and father got divorced and her father lives in New York, while Stacey lives with her mother in Stoneybrook.

Stacey's sophistication shows up not only in the super-responsible and mature way in which she usually acts, but also in the way she dresses. We are pretty casually dressed at the BSC meetings, but even if Stacey is just wearing jeans like most of the rest of us, she goes one step further into cool. For instance, today, when we were wearing sweaters and shirts, Stacey had on an oversized black sweater and a metallic gold T-shirt underneath. With her huge blue eyes and naturally dark lashes, and the shoulder length blonde hair that she keeps perfectly cut, she looked just like a model.

Stacey and Claudia are best friends, which is not surprising, as Claudia has a sense of sophistication and style all her own. But Claudia's sophistication and style are not big city. They're more artistic. Claudia wants to be an artist and is really talented. She works hard on her art and has even had her own art show.

Claudia's bright and talented, but she and school do *not* get along. Somehow, teachers don't appreciate Claudia's "creative" approach to things such as spelling. Claudia has to work really hard to be an average student (at least, an average student grade-wise) at SMS. The Kishis even have a rule that someone in the family has to help Claud with her homework every night.

That's tough, especially as Claudia has an older sister, Janine, who is a genuine genius, but Claudia doesn't let it get to her. She works on her art and keeps her strength up with a truly artistic collection of junk food hidden around her room for BSC meetings and emergencies, such as homework questions. Claudia also really loves Nancy Drew books. As Claud's parents sort of equate Nancy Drew and junk food for some reason, Claudia keeps her collection of Nancy Drew books hidden around her room, too. You might reach behind other books on her bookcase and find a Nancy Drew and a chocolate bar.

Claudia's style is unique. She doesn't often wear jeans, but she was wearing them today—only she'd cut patterns in the legs of the jeans (which were very faded) and was wearing leopard-skin patterned tights underneath so that they showed through. She was wearing her black Doc Martens with yellow shoelaces, and she'd used matching shoelaces to pull her hair back into a long, thick plait. Her earrings were a pair she'd made herself, out of little yellow feathers and black beads. And she was wearing a black and yellow striped flannel shirt buttoned up to her neck, with another pair of shoelaces made into a sort of bow tie.

Nobody but Claudia could wear something like that and look so truly fantastic, not even Stacey. If Stacey looks like a fashion model, Claudia Kishi, with her perfect skin and brown eyes and long hair, sometimes looks like a star. It's amazing.

Claudia is the BSC vice-chairman, and her room is where we hold our meetings, every Monday, Wednesday, and Friday afternoon from five-thirty till six. Claudia is the only one of us with her own phone line, so we can take clients' phone calls and arrange appointments without tying up the phone for the whole family.

You've already met Mallory Pike, so you know she wears glasses and comes from a big family. Mallory has red hair and freckles and wears a brace (at least it's the clear plastic kind). The brace comes off in two years, and meanwhile,

Mallory is working on persuading her parents to let her get contact lenses.

Mallory is a junior officer, like me. Like Kristy, she also has other official duties. Mallory is the secretary of the sixth-grade class at SMS. And, like Claudia and me, she has a career planned as a writer and is already working hard towards her goal. Mal even took two weeks off from the BSC to write a story not too long ago, and won the competition for Best Overall Fiction in the Sixth Grade.

Mallory and I are both different and alike: She's from a big family, I'm from a smaller one. We love reading, especially horse stories. We have English, lunch, gym, and science classes together. But unlike Mary Anne and Kristy, who look rather alike, we don't look alike at all. Mal is shorter than I am, and not athletic, and she has glasses and red hair and pale skin with freckles, while I am tall and thin (a dancer's build) and have black hair and brown eyes and brown skin. (But I do have glasses, just for reading.)

Mal was one of the first people I met when my family moved to Stoneybrook from Oakley, New Jersey, after my father's company transferred him to a new job. I thought at first I was going to *hate* being at SMS, not only because it can be so tough being a new kid in the class, but also because I was the only black student in the sixth grade and one of about six black students in all of SMS. Pretty weird. But after I met Mal and joined the BSC, I stopped feeling like the new girl at school and decided I wasn't going to hate SMS and Stoneybrook after all.

So that's everybody—except Shannon and Logan, our associate members. Associate members don't have to come to meetings. But they are on call for jobs we can't fit into our schedules, and to help out, for instance, when Dawn visited her father and brother in California, or when Mallory was ill with glandular fever, or when Claudia broke her leg because of a practical joke that one of the kids she was babysitting for played, or . . . well, you get the idea.

Shannon lives opposite Kristy, but she doesn't go to SMS, she goes to Stoneybrook Day School. She's a super-serious student and involved in a lot of after-school activities, such as French club and astronomy club. Shannon and Kristy really disliked each other when they first met. Kristy thought Shannon was a complete snob. But they worked things out and Shannon even gave Kristy and her family a puppy, when her dog Astrid, a

Bernese mountain dog, had a litter of puppies. So Shannon and Kristy might even be sort of related—through their dogs!

Logan Bruno is a Southerner, and Mary Anne's boyfriend. Like Mary Anne, he's tough-minded and independent (he got some teasing for being a "boy babysitter" but he didn't let it get to him). When he's not playing baseball and being involved in other sports, he comes to meetings occasionally and he's a great babysitter. And while I don't think he looks *exactly* like the film star Cam Geary, as Mary Anne does, I do think he's pretty cute.

Back to the club. We were having a busy day. The phone would start ringing almost the moment we hung up, and Mary Anne was kept busy scheduling appointments in the club record book. The record book contains clients' names, addresses, phone numbers, rates paid, special information we might need, and all the schedules of babysitting jobs. Mary Anne is in charge of the entire record book except for Stacey's treasury section. (And she's never, *ever* made a mistake in scheduling.)

Meanwhile, the rest of us were handing round the BSC notebook, writing in it, and reading the new entries. The club notebook helps us keep up with our clients (someone's going through the terrible twos, someone else has developed an allergy) as well as giving us an insight into how to handle difficult situations that might come up. We grumble, but we all keep up with reading *and* writing in the notebook.

I'd just finished reading about Jackie Rodowsky's latest disaster, involving a carpet, a bowl of goldfish, and a boiled egg—Jackie is one of our favourite kids, but trouble follows him wherever he goes—when I heard Kristy say, "That's great, Mrs Roberts. Yes. Yes, we'll call you right back."

"Mrs Roberts?" I asked as she rang off. "Danielle's mother?"

Kristy nodded with a big grin on her face. "Yes. She's wondering if anyone would be interested in sitting for Danielle, and Greg, of course, next Wednesday afternoon. Now who would want that job? Mary Anne, can you check the record book and see who's free that day?"

"Kristy!" I said indignantly, before I realized she was teasing, and then we all started laughing.

Everyone knew about Danielle, from when I worked at the Kids Club. She'd been a member of the Kids Club, but before I started volunteering, she'd had to go into hospital for treatment for leukaemia. When I eventually met her, she'd just got out of hospital. She was a skinny kid with huge brown eyes, wearing a scarf on her head that didn't quite hide the fact that the chemotherapy treatments she'd had in the hospital had made her lose her hair. She was also wearing a T-shirt that said "Bald is Beautiful".

See? Who wouldn't find a kid like Danielle really cool?

I'd even helped make one of Danielle's two wishes come true. She'd always wanted to visit Disney World, so I put her family in touch with an organization called Your Wish Is My Command, which tries to grant the wishes of kids with serious illnesses.

And Danielle and her mother and father and six-and-a-half-year-old brother Greg all got to go to Disney World for three whole days!

But I couldn't help Danielle with her other wish: to get through primary school. There was no guarantee that Danielle would ever get cured, or even get better. There was no guarantee what would ever happen. And in fact, when I'd ended my work at the Kids Club, just after Danielle came back from Disney World, she had to go back in the hospital for more tests and treatments.

Danielle spent a lot of time in the hospital. But now she's in remission. These days, Danielle doesn't look so skinny and she's full of energy. Her hair has grown back (in a different colour, sort of red) so she looks just like an ordinary kid with a short haircut.

Danielle is nine, a year older than Becca and Char, but she doesn't say "almost" ten when you ask her how old she is. She says nine and she says it proudly, as if she's achieved a special goal.

And she has.

You see why Kristy's teasing made me indignant? Of course I wanted to be the one to sit for Danielle and Greg!

Mary Anne flipped through the pages of the record book. "Hmmm," she said. "You might be able to work it in, Jessi."

"I think you'd better take the job, then," said Mal, giving me a friendly poke on the shoulder.

I rolled my eyes, but I was grinning, too, as Kristy picked up the phone to call Mrs Roberts back.

The BSC had a new client—one of the greatest kids I knew.

# 3rd
# CHAPTER

When I arrived at the Robertses' house, I heard Danielle shriek, "I'll get it! It's Jessi!" A moment later the door opened wide and Danielle stood there, grinning from ear to ear.

"Jessi!" she shouted, as if she hadn't seen me for ages. Naturally that made me feel good. I didn't shriek, too, though. I tried to remember that I was a grown-up, responsible babysitter. I just grinned as widely as Danielle and said, "How are you?"

"Grrreat!" replied Danielle loudly. She sounded excited about something, but before I could ask any questions she sang out, "Mummm, it's Jessi!" and raced halfway down the hall before stopping to slide to the end in her stocking feet. She caught herself on the edge of a doorway, swung around it, and disappeared.

33

Mrs Roberts came out of the study and said, (in a calmer tone), "Jessi, it's good to see you." She looked down at the pen she was holding, put it behind her ear, and reached out to shake hands with me.

"It's good to see you, too," I said. I looked at Mrs Roberts and suddenly realized where Danielle's new red hair might have come from. Mrs Roberts' own hair, which she wore in a short, sleek style, was the same soft shade of red-brown.

"Danielle's looking good," I said as I stepped into the house.

Mrs Roberts smiled. "She really is, isn't she? She's got so much energy, so much spirit. Even more than before she—got ill. She's doing very, very well."

"That's great," I said. I took that to mean that Danielle really was feeling better. Maybe this was more than a remission. Maybe . . .

But I stopped myself. One day at a time. It was enough for today that Danielle felt good.

Mrs Roberts rooted around in the hall cupboard and pulled out a puffy parka and a shoulder bag, which she slung over her shoulder. She unhooked car keys from a key rack by the cupboard and said, "I'll be gone for about an hour and a half. I have to get the car inspected and as I need new tyres, I booked that for today, too. The number for the car service centre is on the notepad by the telephone. There are also the numbers of Mr Roberts at his office, the fire brigade, the police station, and the hospital. And of course, Danielle's doctor. Not that you'll be needing any of these."

"I hope not!" I said.

"You've been here before, so you know your way around the house. We're having an early dinner tonight, so Danielle and Greg can have a snack, but only a small one—a piece of fruit or one or two biscuits out of the jar on the kitchen worktop, and some juice or milk."

"Are there any, I mean, is there anything Danielle can't do?" I asked. I hoped I didn't sound stupid. I knew that when Danielle was feeling ill, she had to rest a lot and take naps and she couldn't race around and tire herself out. But I didn't quite know how to ask about that.

Mrs Roberts didn't seem to think the question was a silly one. In fact, she understood just what I meant.

"Danielle's been very active these days, with no ill effects," she told me. "We're trying to let her enjoy using her energy as much as possible. So yes, keep an eye on her and if she looks pale or tired, make her sit down and rest. But don't be too protective. Use your best judgement." She paused, then added, "The same goes for Greg!"

"Right," I said.

Mrs Roberts looked at her watch. "Whoops! I'll be late if I don't hurry. See you soon."

I was pleased that Mrs Roberts was so thorough. Some clients are not, and that makes it harder to be a good babysitter.

When Mrs Roberts had left, I went down the hall and looked into the room where Danielle had disappeared. She and Greg were lying on their stomachs, watching their kitten, Mr Toes, chase a catnip mouse. (Mr Toes is all grey with white feet, which is why Greg called him Mr Toes.)

"Hey, cat lady," I said. "Hey, cat gentleman."

Danielle giggled. "Isn't Mr Toes the *cutest* cat?" she asked.

Mr Toes picked up the mouse, flipped it in the air, and then ran sideways in a display of extra-cuteness.

"Yup," I said. "The cutest." I bent down and flicked the mouse towards him and we all laughed as he pounced and then skittered away.

Greg said, "I've got a new book about a cat. Can I read it to you, Jessi?"

"Okay," I said. "Danielle, what about you? What do you want to do?"

"I don't want to do my homework, that's for sure," said Danielle. "But I suppose I should get it over with so I can play."

"Good idea," I said, impressed. "Why don't you work on that for a while, and then we can all do something together?"

"Okay." Danielle jumped up and went to her room. Greg got his beginners' reading book and sat down next to me. It was a mystery involving a cat, and the illustrations were funny.

"I've never seen this one before," I told Greg. "It looks good."

"It is," he said. "Now, shhh! Listen while I read."

Hiding a smile, I said, "Okay. Go ahead."

We read the cat mystery and then I pulled out one of my favourites, a book about a pair of friends called *Frog and Toad*, and we read that one. We were just about to start on a Dr Seuss book when I heard an enormous crash from the back of the house.

"Good grief!" I said, jumping up so fast I dropped all the books. I raced towards the noise with Greg right behind me.

Danielle was lying sprawled on the floor of the study with a small bookcase tipped over beside her and books all over the floor.

"Danielle!" I cried. "Are you all right?"

Sitting up, Danielle said, "Ooops!"

"Don't move," I said, visions of broken bones dancing in my head. "Does it hurt anywhere?"

"No," said Danielle, giving me a funny look. I suddenly realized that I might be overreacting just a little.

"Nothing hurts?" I said, just to be sure.

"No," replied Danielle.

I started to help her to her feet—and then I saw the Rollerblades.

"What are you doing wearing Rollerblades in the house?" I asked.

"Those are Mum's!" exclaimed Greg.

"Yes. They're too big for me. I think that's why I fell over," said Danielle.

The blades *were* too big—far too big. They looked enormous at the end of Danielle's long, thin legs.

I took a deep breath. I couldn't believe that Danielle had been skating in the house. On the other hand, was it really that big a deal? The weather hadn't been good enough to skate outside, or even to go out to work off all the wild, full-of-life energy Danielle was clearly enjoying these days.

Danielle bent over and began unlacing the blades. "I wish I could get a pair of my own. Mum and Dad both have a pair, but all I have are my old roller skates. They said I have to wait till I'm feeling a little better. But I *am* feeling better now."

"You should probably wait till spring, anyway," I said. "Then you can try them outside."

"*If* I ever get any," said Danielle. She looked up. "I want to learn to skate really *fast*."

The idea didn't appeal to me at all. I'd seen how fast those Rollerblades could go (Kristy's a pro at it). Even wearing all the protective gear, helmets and kneepads and wrist braces and elbow pads, I could just imagine what one fast fall could do. Like completely wreck a knee or an arm— not something a ballet dancer wants to do!

I didn't say that, of course, I didn't even say anything about Danielle sneaking her mother's skates out and trying to skate in the house. It could have been a disaster, but apart from a few books scattered around, no harm had been done.

I helped Danielle get out of her mum's

Rollerblades and the three of us lifted the bookshelf upright and put the books back in place. Then we went to the kitchen for a snack. We made crazy fruit salad (bananas, apples and pears cut into different shapes) and drank milk. We'd just finished when Mrs Roberts came back.

"How did it go?" she said cheerfully, coming in the door. "No problems, I hope."

What could I say? I didn't think Mrs Roberts would be upset by the Rollerblade incident and in a way, it was sort of funny. I'd leave it to Danielle to tell her mother.

"Everything went fine," I said.

"I made banana monster fruit salad," said Greg. "See?"

Mrs Roberts laughed. "Good," she said. "Thanks, Jessi."

"No problem," I said. "No problem at all."

# 4th CHAPTER

Sun, no snow, and a quick walk home from school helped to keep my muscles stretched. I'd felt a little sluggish that morning when I'd got up to practise at the *barre*, and I didn't want it to become a habit.

Maybe when I got home I'd do a little work at the *barre*, just to make sure I'd shaken off the morning dance blahs.

But when I reached my house, I slowed down. A car I didn't recognize was parked in the drive. Did we have visitors? Was it someone I knew? Or a friend of Aunt Cecelia's I'd have to sit with and be polite to?

Maybe I wouldn't get to do any *barre* work after all.

I went into the house and the first thing I saw was Becca in the hall.

41

"Becca?" I asked.

She was crouched over in a funny huddle. When she heard me, she looked over her shoulder and said, very softly, "Shhhhhhh!"

I lowered my voice to a whisper. "Why?"

She pointed at her ear and at the door, then went back to her huddled position. I realized that she had pressed her ear against the closed door of the living room.

Becca was eavesdropping through the keyhole!

I was instantly intrigued. As an older sister who was supposed to set a good example, I suppose I should have said something like, "You shouldn't eavesdrop. It's wrong."

But as a person who likes mysteries, I couldn't help but recognize the mystery potential in the situation. I mean, it wasn't like Becca to eavesdrop. So she must have had a good reason.

All these thoughts went through my mind in a flash. And while I was thinking them, my body was doing a perfect *glissade* forward into a position new to the world of ballet: the eavesdroppers' crouch.

At first I couldn't hear anything. Then a deep, rumbly voice laughed, followed by a familiar, husky chuckle. The chuckle was Aunt Cecelia. I didn't recognize the laugh. But it belonged to a man.

". . . something new," said the male voice.

"Something borrowed and something blue," came Aunt Cecelia's voice. "I'll see what . . ."

Her voice faded out and I frowned with concentration. Where had I heard those words before? And recently?

"A spring theme . . ." Aunt Cecelia's voice said again. ". . . daffodils, lilacs . . ."

". . . catered?" said the man's voice.

This was *frustrating*. No wonder people say you aren't supposed to eavesdrop. It could drive you crazy!

Then Becca reached out, clutched the edge of my sweater, and yanked hard. I almost toppled over. But not just because of the yank that Becca had given me. I'd heard the same words she had heard, loud and clear.

My aunt Cecelia's voice, saying, "Oh, I can hardly wait. We're going to have a lovely wedding!"

Of course! "Something old, something new, something borrowed, something blue." We were about to have a wedding!

I straightened up and grabbed Becca's shoulder. She stood up, her eyes lit up with excitement, her hand over her mouth.

I put a finger over my lips. "Shh! Come on!" We beat a hasty retreat to my room. The moment I closed my door, Becca flung herself on my bed and bounced up and down.

"I can't believe it," she cried. "A wedding! Aunt Cecelia's getting married!"

"I can't believe it, either!" I gasped. "Aunt Cecelia! I didn't even know she was going out with anybody! Did you?"

Becca shook her head. "But she has been awfully busy lately. Maybe that's what she's been doing. Seeing this man, I mean."

"Did he just propose?" I wondered.

Becca said, "I don't know. Oooh! Wouldn't *that* be exciting? I might have been listening to a *proposal*."

"Did you see who it was, Becca? Did you hear anything else?"

Becca shook her head again, regretfully. "No. I got home just before you did. I went in the back door and I didn't see Aunt Cecelia, so I called out, 'I'm home!' And I heard Aunt Cecelia in the hall and she said, 'That's Becca. Go on in and make yourself comfortable.' So I went into the hall and Aunt Cecelia was standing outside the living room door and she said, 'Becca, this is Mr Major. And this is my niece Rebecca. Now, Becca, when

Jessi gets home there're freshly baked oat-meal raisin biscuits in the oven and you can each have two. I'm busy right now.' And she closed the living room door. And just before she closed it I heard this man's voice say something I didn't under-stand."

"So you wanted to find out what was going on?"

Becca grinned. "Of course! But before I could really hear anything, you got home."

I thought for a moment, then said, "Too bad. I mean, I don't think he had time to propose to Aunt Cecelia. So it must have happened before."

"And now they're planning their wed-ding." Becca hugged herself in excite-ment. "I *love* weddings. Do you think we'll get to be in it?"

I didn't answer. I sat down at my desk, thinking fast and hard. Finally I said, "You know what this means? Aunt Cece-lia won't be living with us any more. We'll have to get someone to look after Squirt. And . . . you and I will probably have a lot more responsibility."

I didn't say what else I was thinking, which was: more freedom. I liked Aunt Cecelia, but she was still strict and kept a sharp eye on all of us. On the whole that's a good thing. As a babysitter, I could understand that. But as a person who had outgrown babysitters, I didn't feel I needed someone to keep a strict watch over me.

Of course there were other important things to think about. For instance, if we were bridesmaids, what would our dresses look like? Would we get to choose the colours? Was Squirt old enough to be in the wedding? (I tried for a moment to imagine Squirt in a little suit, dressed up as a ring bearer. The image of Squirt in a suit was really cute, until I also imagined him putting the ring in his mouth and swallowing it.)

I looked at Becca. "Do you, Jessi?" she repeated. "Do you think we'll get to be in Aunt Cecelia's wedding?"

"I don't know," I said, "but even if we're not *in* it, we'll have to dress up specially for it."

"When do you think we'll find out? Shall we ask Aunt Cecelia?"

I thought about that for a moment. "Nooo, I don't think so. I mean, I think it must be a secret or she would have told us. Besides, if we ask her she'll know . . ."

". . . that I was eavesdropping," finished Becca. She looked a little worried. The idea of telling our aunt that we'd been eavesdropping wasn't at all pleasant.

"I was eavesdropping, too," I said quickly, to reassure Becca that she wasn't in this alone. "Anyway, I'm sure she'll tell us soon enough. I mean, how could she keep such amazing news a secret?"

We grinned. Amazing hardly described it. The news needed a Karen Brewer word—gigundoly.

So Aunt Cecelia was getting married. *When* had it all happened? Was that really why she'd been so busy lately?

The members of the BSC have wedding experience from babysitter to bridesmaid. But that didn't matter. I knew that no matter how many weddings I was involved in, I was always going to find them super-exciting.

Especially at a time like this, when my own aunt was going to be the bride. Wait till I told everyone in the BSC! Wait till Mama and Daddy found out. Or did they already know?

But I could think about that later. Becca and I had more important things to think about just then.

"When do you think we can go shopping?" I asked Becca. "What are we going to wear?"

# 5th CHAPTER

Tuesday

Danielle really is feeling — and looking — better. And all that new energy is making her, well, very creative. And that's great. I think...

When Mary Anne reached the Robertses' house, she was practically in a state of shock. She hadn't planned on working that day—at least not babysitting.

Had Mary Anne done the unimaginable and made a mistake in the club record book? Had she forgotten to schedule an appointment, or scheduled one at the wrong time?

No. But not quite an hour earlier, she'd picked up the phone to hear Stacey's breathless voice: "Mannecanyouhelpmeou?"

At least, that's what it sounded like to Mary Anne. "Stacey!" she gasped. "What's wrong?"

"I—it's just that I'm supposed to sit for the Robertses in an hour and I can't." Stacey ended the sentence on what was, for Stacey, a sort of wail.

Mary Anne did a quick mental flip through her calendar for the afternoon, shifted her plan to begin work on a social studies paper to later in the evening, and said, "Oh. Is there anything I can do to help?"

So Stacey jumped in and explained what the emergency was, right? Wrong. She said, "I'll call the Robertses. Thankyouthankyouthank*you*."

And rang off.

Wow! thought Mary Anne, and started getting organized for an afternoon with the Robertses. Naturally, being Mary Anne, that included phoning the Robertses first and confirming with them that she was replacing Stacey for the afternoon.

So Mrs Roberts didn't look surprised when she opened the door. "Hi, Mary Anne," she said cheerfully. Her voice was loud. That was because a deafening cacophony was coming from the back of the house.

"Hi, Mrs Roberts!" answered Mary Anne just as loudly.

Mrs Roberts pulled on her jacket and made a face. "The children are feeling cooped up," she explained. "Even though Danielle is feeling so much better, I don't want her to go out and play in this weather. She was really keen to try some tobogganing, even though there's not enough snow on the ground to do much of that. Anyway, we're trying to give her and Greg plenty of leeway to work off their high spirits indoors. Right now they're playing doctor."

"Excuse me?" said Mary Anne, startled.

"Danielle is Dr Frankenstein, the evil scientist doctor, and Greg is her assistant, Nurse Igor."

"Right," said Mary Anne, swallowing hard and forcing herself to listen as Mrs Roberts went over the phone numbers and instructions for the afternoon.

"I'll be back in about an hour and a half, but Mr Roberts may beat me home," Mrs Roberts concluded.

"Right," said Mary Anne again. She could hear the wild cries of "Dr Frankenstein!"

Good grief! she thought. She knew Danielle had spent a lot of time in hospitals, but she hadn't expected this!

She walked cautiously towards the playroom. "Dr Frankenstein" came tearing out wearing a white baseball hat and an oversized white bathrobe that flapped around her ankles, and carrying a big jar.

"Eeek!" said Mary Anne. "What's in the jar?"

"It's my specimen jar," said Danielle, grinning ghoulishly.

"Yeah," said Greg (who for some reason was wearing a cowboy hat).

Mary Anne felt herself turning green. The jar was filled with something evil-coloured and icky-looking. She was afraid to ask.

"Er, Danielle," she began.

Greg began to laugh. "She believed you, she believed you, Dr Frank!"

Mary Anne's face turned from green to red. She almost *had* believed Danielle.

Danielle started laughing and turned from the fiendish Dr Frankenstein back into herself. "It's leftover pea soup with ketchup and a chopped-up hot dog," she explained.

"Right," said Mary Anne. That was still pretty gross, but in spite of her red face, she began to grin, too. "So, er, do you want to keep playing doctor? Maybe we could do something else."

"Okay," said Danielle.

"Okay," echoed Greg happily. "What?"

"Can I phone Charlotte and Haley and see if they can come over to play?" asked Danielle.

"I don't see why not," said Mary Anne. Mrs Roberts hadn't said Danielle had homework to finish. And it *was* great to see her with so much energy.

"Cool," said Danielle and exited at hyper-speed to use the phone, her white coat flapping behind her, her "specimen jar" under her arm.

Greg said, "Is that your Kid-Kit?"

Mary Anne looked down at the box under *her* arm. "Yes," she said. "How did you know?"

Greg shrugged. "I heard," he said.

"Do you want to see what's in it?"

Greg nodded.

Danielle, Greg and Mary Anne went through the contents of the Kid-Kit until Charlotte and Haley arrived. Then Mary Anne and Greg settled down with a book that instantly caught Greg's attention, *Freckle Juice*, while Charlotte, Haley and Danielle disappeared into Danielle's room.

It was quiet for a while. In spite of the short notice and the rush to get to the Robertses', Mary Anne began to feel mellow.

Until it happened.

Not a disaster on the Jackie Rodowsky scale, exactly. Not an accident, either. It was actually a pretty interesting idea—if you weren't the babysitter.

It started with an odd whump-thumping. At first Mary Anne thought it was the pipes or just the random winter sounds a house makes. It wasn't enough to make her instincts go on alert.

When she heard it again, she wondered if a storm door was banging or a shutter was loose on the house. She decided to check.

"Excuse me for just a minute," she said to Greg.

The thumping was louder in the hall. And it was accompanied by muffled voices.

Mary Anne followed the sounds to the basement door. She heard a shriek, a giggle, and more thumping. She pulled the door open and found herself in—

Aspen, Colorado.

Not really. But Danielle, Charlotte and Haley *had* brought a little of the great outdoors inside.

They were tobogganing down the basement stairs. Using what looked like the mattress from a cot.

As Mary Anne opened the door, Charlotte took off, thumping and bumping down the stairs. She landed at the bottom with a muffled shriek and Danielle's voice said, "Amazing, Char. You went almost all the way to the boiler."

"My turn," Haley's voice said. "Help me carry the toboggan back up the sta . . ." Her voice trailed off. She had spotted Mary Anne.

"Ahem!" said Mary Anne.

The three girls came sheepishly to the bottom of the stairs.

"That's my mattress!" said Greg, who of course had followed Mary Anne.

"It's your old mattress, Greg. From when you were a baby. You don't use it any more," said Danielle.

The three girls looked guilty, but pleased with themselves.

They also looked completely filthy. They were covered with soot from the basement boiler, and dust and dirt and cobwebs.

The stairs were steep and the basement floor was hard and uneven. From where she was standing, Mary Anne could see rakes and hoes and even an old-fashioned lawn-mower with rotary blades. What if the mattress had crashed into that? What if one of them had fallen on the blades? Or what if the mattress had turned over halfway down the stairs?

Mary Anne closed her eyes. She took a deep breath. None of that happened, she reminded herself.

"Leave the mattress," she said. "And come up here and let's see about getting you lot cleaned up."

"We'll put it back where we found it," said Haley helpfully and she and Char wrestled the mattress into a sort of standing position against a basement wall.

"Fine," said Mary Anne. "Come on."

The girls emerged from the basement looking as if they'd been potholing.

Mary Anne reached out and touched Danielle's arm. The soot was oily and sticky. It was going to take forever to get it off.

"Our boiler broke down this winter and

it made soot go all over the basement before they got it mended," said Danielle happily.

Mary Anne found towels (dark ones) and sent Danielle, Haley and Charlotte to the bathroom to clean up. She'd just got them passable (and the bathroom cleaned up) when she heard the front door open.

"Mum!" shouted Danielle. She didn't seem particularly worried or upset about the tobogganing incident, and Mary Anne had a feeling that Mrs Roberts would just laugh it off. She decided to let Danielle and Greg be the ones to do the talking.

After all, it hadn't been so terrible. And nothing bad had happened. Okay, so maybe Danielle was pushing the limits a little. She must have known that what she was doing wasn't on the parent-and-baby-sitter-approved list.

But you couldn't blame her for trying it out. And for wanting to pack every activity that she had missed while she was in the hospital, into these newfound days of feeling good.

What would Stacey have done? wondered Mary Anne as she made her way home. And what was going on with Stacey?

Oh, well. She'd find out soon enough.

She passed some kids on pieces of cardboard, trying to toboggan down a muddy, gullied section of hill in their front garden.

She watched them for a minute, then shook her head, smiling ruefully, and headed for home.

# 6th
# CHAPTER

I made a *grand jeté* through the door of Claudia's room, but it was no use. I was late. All thanks to traffic and my father's driving. (He *always* stops for yellow lights. That's a good thing, don't get me wrong. But not when I'm on my way from dance class at Mme Noelle's to the BSC meeting at Claudia's.)

Kristy made a point of checking the time on her watch. I knew what it said: 5:32.

She gave me her Look.

"Sorry," I said, and slid into a seat on the floor next to Mallory.

Mallory gave me a sympathetic grin and the bag of marshmallows she'd been holding.

The phone rang and Claudia picked it up. "Babysitters Club," she said.

I looked around the room—and was suddenly indignant. I didn't deserve the Look. I wasn't the only one who was late. Stacey was late, too. Later than me. She hadn't even arrived yet.

"Mrs Rodowsky needs a sitter for Jackie for next Friday night," said Claudia.

Mary Anne flipped open the record book.

And I said to Mallory, "Where's Stacey?"

Mallory shrugged.

Claudia frowned down at the bag of pretzels lying unopened on her desk. They were unopened because 1) as junk food, pretzels do not appeal to Claudia. 2) junk food without sugar is the only kind of junk food Stacey can eat—and the only kind Dawn will eat as she doesn't believe in eating junk food. 3) Dawn had brought a low-fat trail mix that she'd made herself. It was actually pretty good.

So the pretzels weren't open. And by the time Dawn had been assigned the Rodowsky job, and by the time Kristy had called Mrs Rodowsky back with the information, they were still unopened. This was because Stacey *still* hadn't arrived.

Claudia said, "She hasn't even phoned. Stacey, I mean. I hope nothing's wrong."

She was beginning to look worried, and

I wasn't surprised. If I got to a BSC meeting and Mallory weren't there, and I hadn't heard from her, I'd be worried, too. I'd think, why didn't she tell me she wasn't coming? Why hasn't she phoned? That's not like Mallory. Oh, my lord, what if something's happened to her? What if she's hurt and can't phone? What if no one knows where she is? What if . . .

Maybe I'm more like Aunt Cecelia than I thought. After all, when my aunt first started living with us, she wanted me to phone home if I were going to be even just a few minutes late.

But Mallory's my best friend, so it would be only natural that I would worry, right? And only natural that Claudia would worry, too, as Stacey is her best friend.

Kristy didn't look worried. Our fearless leader kept checking her watch and frowning. Every once in a while she'd give a little snort. It sounded rather ominous. I was glad I wasn't Stacey. Getting a Look from Kristy was one thing. But I had a feeling Kristy was really going to let Stacey have it.

The phone rang again and I grabbed the notebook and glanced through the pages. I had just got to Mary Anne's entry when Kristy said (with a little snort), "Well, what happened, Mary Anne? How did it go with Danielle?"

I put my finger in the book to mark my place and looked up. Mary Anne said, "Wellll, Danielle does seem to be feeling better these days. A lot better."

"Doesn't she?" I said eagerly. "She's got so much energy! And she looks great."

Everyone smiled at that. It was good news. But Mary Anne's next words made us a little more thoughtful.

"She does look great," agreed Mary Anne. "But—well, let me tell you what she did when I was sitting for her on Tuesday."

Some of us had already read what Mary Anne had written in the notebook, of course. But I hadn't, and besides, the notebook didn't go into all the details that Mary Anne did.

"Wow!" said Kristy, when Mary Anne had finished. The rest of us were dumbfounded, too.

"It's not that Danielle did a *terrible* thing," said Mary Anne. "I mean, it's kind of logical in a way."

Claudia nodded thoughtfully. "True. And it's not as though she's trying to be the worst kid ever, or anything."

"Yes," said Kristy, who had had an

experience with a kid we had actually called "the worst kid ever".

Mallory said, "I know it's not the same thing, but when I was getting over glandular fever, the first day I felt really good, I wanted to go crazy. I mean, it was wonderful. I felt as if I was going to burst. I bet Danielle, after all she's been through, feels that way about a million times more."

I looked at Mallory gratefully. She understood. And she'd put into words exactly what I'd been feeling. But . . .

I sighed. "She was kind of out of control when I sat for her, too," I confessed. "She got hold of her mum's Rollerblades—"

"Her *mum* has Rollerblades?" asked Claudia. "Coool."

"Didn't you read about it in the notebook?" Kristy asked Claudia sternly. (I think Kristy was a little touchy because Stacey still hadn't turned up—or phoned.)

Claudia was unabashed. "I might have missed a few words," she said cheerfully. "So go on about the Rollerblades."

I told my friends about the skating incident. "It wasn't a major disaster or anything," I concluded, "so I just let it go."

"Me, too." Mary Anne nodded. "I mean, Mrs Roberts was so glad that Danielle was feeling well. And she told me before I left that she was in high spirits. I got the feeling that she'd just consider this her high spirits."

"Maybe we should forget about it," I said. "I mean, Danielle has worked so hard. She's been in the hospital more than she's been out of it lately. She must feel as if she's making up for lost time and lost life."

We were silent for a moment. Then Dawn nodded slowly. "You're right. Besides, if her parents aren't concerned, I don't think we should be."

"Right," said Kristy, looking relieved. Her brisk tone dispelled the choked-up feeling that I could sense was coming over my friends (especially Mary Anne, who was looking a little teary-eyed.)

"So," I said quickly. "Listen to this, everyone. There's going to be another wedding!"

Everyone shrieked at once, and I told them how Becca and I had accidentally-on-purpose overheard Aunt Cecelia planning a wedding with Mr Major.

"Are you going to be in the wedding?" asked Mary Anne, her romantic instincts taking over.

"What are you going to wear?" asked Claudia.

"Are you going to have to wear a dress?" added Kristy, looking alarmed and disgusted at the same time.

"I'll be glad to help work out some healthy, yummy food for the wedding," said Dawn.

Mal grinned a big, huge Mallory grin. "Aunt Cecelia, huh? That's going to be *some* wedding!"

We burst out laughing and then plunged headlong into wedding plans and speculation, hardly even pausing when the phone rang and we arranged babysitting appointments.

Except for when the phone rang at three minutes to six and Kristy answered it.

"Stacey!" she cried. "Where are you? What's wrong?"

Everyone fell silent at once.

"I *know* you can't get to the meeting," said Kristy. "Honestly, Stacey! It's almost six o'clock now."

She was frowning, and she frowned even harder as she listened.

"No," she said. "But Stacey? Well, goodbye to you, too."

Kristy rang off. "That was Stacey," she said. Her frown looked as if it were about to become permanent.

64

"What's wrong?" asked Claudia.

Kristy shook her head. Her lips were thin. Our fearless leader looked pretty fearsome. And pretty annoyed.

"She didn't say. She just said she was sorry, that she couldn't get to the meeting. And that she had to go."

Wow! No one in the history of the BSC (okay, maybe I'm exaggerating, but you get the idea) had ever just written off a meeting like that. Especially not to Kristy.

We all kept quiet.

Then Kristy looked at her watch. "Meeting adjourned," she barked. And after getting up, she stomped out of the door.

# 7th CHAPTER

"Shop till you drop," I whispered, pushing open the front door of the mall.

"Here comes the briiide," Becca sang, under her breath and way off-key.

We giggled.

It was Saturday afternoon, grey and windy and perfect for not doing anything out-of-doors. So Becca and I had decided it was time to shop for dresses for Aunt Cecelia's wedding, as well as maybe something special for Squirt. Aunt Cecelia had made it extra easy for us, because she'd decided she was going to Washington Mall "to do a little browsing".

I'd been sitting next to Becca at breakfast when Aunt Cecelia had made that announcement and I'd elbowed Becca so hard she'd almost fallen off the chair.

"Could we come, too?" I said aloud. "Unless, of course, there's something *special* that you need to shop for that's a secret."

Now was Aunt Cecelia's big chance to tell us All. But she didn't. She said, "I like shopping at my own pace. But you can come with me. You can shop together and then we'll make arrangements to meet afterwards."

"Sounds like fun," Mama had said, smiling at both of us.

Becca nudged me back and said, "It certainly does."

Washington Mall was the biggest mall around, five whole levels of shopping half an hour from Stoneybrook.

Aunt Cecelia gave us a list of dos and don'ts and rules and regulations that was about a mile long. As she'd been going over the same list in the car, we knew it pretty well. Besides, it was basic safety and manners stuff. "Don't talk to strangers. Don't get separated. Be polite. Always say please and thank you."

But we nodded and said, "Yes, Aunt Cecelia," politely. We didn't want to blow our chance to do some wedding shopping (just like Aunt Cecelia was doing, we *knew*).

"We will meet back right here in an

hour and a half," Aunt Cecelia said. "Coordinate watches."

We coordinated watches. "Behave," said Aunt Cecelia, and strode away into the crowd.

"Do you think they'll have one of those sweet little dinner jackets for babies?" said Becca as we plunged into our shopping expedition.

"I hope so," I said. "We mustn't forget a wedding present for Aunt Cecelia and Mr Major either."

"But let's go to the baby shop first."

"Okay. We'll look there first."

Unfortunately, Baby Look At You Now! (the Washington Mall baby shop) didn't have any little dinner jackets for Squirt, but when we told the assistant our brother was going to be a member of a wedding—a very important wedding— she came up with all kinds of cute outfits, including a baby suit jacket and a shirt with a soft little red bow tie attached to it.

"This is *soo* cute," said Becca.

"You could take it home and try it out on him," suggested the assistant, "and return it in exchange for something else if it doesn't fit. Or a different size."

"Ooooh!" said Becca.

But I remembered just how much

money we had for our shopping trip and pulled Becca away in time. "We'll bring Squirt with us the next time," I promised over my shoulder as we left the shop.

"Don't forget how much money we *don't* have to spend right now," I warned Becca as we strolled back out into the mall.

"I know, I know. You said this is the preliminary shopping expedition," she replied.

"Right. We look, we compare, we narrow our choices. We focus." (I could almost hear Mme Noelle saying that to me in dance class: "You must *focus*. It is ze important thing.")

"Right," Becca said back to me, nodding solemnly. Then she giggled. "Can we look in Steven E's?"

"Of course," I said, grinning. Steven E's was *the* most expensive store in Washington Mall. "We'll go to Laura Ashley's, too. But we'd better look at Penney's and Macy's, too. It's important that we consider a wide range of possibilities. Let's start at a department store first. We can look at wedding gifts there, too."

So we did. We tried on dresses at Penney's (and visited their bridal department). We wandered through the home furnishings department. (Becca fell in love with a lamp. I can't exactly describe it except to say that I didn't think it was quite right for a wedding present. Although, of course, Aunt Cecelia might need some new home furnishings when she and Mr Major moved into their own house.)

"But they might move into Mr Major's house," I pointed out, practically dragging Becca away from The Lamp. "And you don't know how it's decorated. This might not go with his stuff at all."

"Oh," said Becca. She sounded disappointed.

"And she's got lots of stuff in storage from when she moved in with us, remember?"

"Oh, right. I suppose we'll have to find something else."

"We will," I promised.

Next we tried on perfume (it doesn't hurt to smell good for a wedding, too) and discussed which would be better from which season and time of day.

"Like if it's an evening wedding," I said, "we'll want something more glamorous."

"Or if it's a formal wedding," agreed Becca.

"But if it's in June and it's hot outside, nothing too heavy."

"Like this!" shrieked Becca, spraying something really strong on my wrist.

"Ugh!" I gasped. I looked up and noticed the assistant giving us the eye and said, "Thank you for the sample, Becca. But I don't think this is what we're looking for." I took Becca's arm and we walked away in a very dignified, adult manner. But when we were out of sight of the perfume counter, we collapsed, giggling.

"Peee-youuuuu! You stink." Becca held her nose.

"So do you," I said, holding my own nose.

Next we found a couple of good possibilities for Becca but nothing for me. At least, nothing I could afford. I found one terrific pale pink dress that had "wedding" written all over it. But the price had "no way" written on it, too.

"It looks super, Jessi," said Becca, who'd been twirling in front of the mirror in a satiny yellow dress.

"Yes. And it would be perfect with a hat."

"Maybe it'll get marked down by the time the wedding comes," said Becca. "After all, we don't know when it's going to be yet."

"True. And that would give me time to save up for it." I felt better. I took the dress off (reluctantly) and then hung it at the end of the rack where people would be less likely to find it.

"I'm hungry," said Becca.

"Let's go to Casa Grande," I said. "Mal and I love the Super Burrito."

"I'm not sure I'm that hungry," said Becca.

"We can share one," I said. "And we'll go to Donut Delite for dessert."

"Cool," said Becca.

It felt good to sit down at Casa Grande. We'd been shopping for a long time. It was almost time to meet Aunt Cecelia.

And I was so tired, I was actually looking forward to it. I was ready to lean back in the car and rest my feet.

"You know what?" said Becca thoughtfully. "Maybe we don't have to get them *things* for a wedding gift. Maybe we could get them something like tickets to a play or passes to the cinema for when they get back."

"Hey, that's a great idea!" I said. We talked about the wedding for a while, and ways we could get information about it without giving away that we knew what was going on. It was rather strange that Aunt Cecelia hadn't said *anything* to us at all, but maybe she had told Mama and Daddy, and was just waiting for the right time to let

Becca and me in on it. We wondered if parents could be in weddings. Could our parents be the best man and the bridesmaid (or bridesmatron?). We knew, as Aunt Cecelia had been married before, that she probably wouldn't do the long white dress thing. But what would she wear?

"We could ask at Rita's Bridal Shoppe," suggested Becca.

"Another great idea!" I exclaimed.

Becca grinned and slurped her Coke noisily. "Not as good as some of Danielle's! She thinks up the *best* things, Jessi. You wouldn't believe them."

Yes, I would, I thought, remembering the Rollerblades in the house and turning the basement stairs into a giant toboggan run. But I didn't say anything aloud.

"Really," Becca went on. "She's very, well, you know, creative. And her parents just laugh, instead of like, getting angry when one of her great ideas doesn't quite work out."

Translation: Danielle was getting away with a lot.

"You have great ideas of your own," I said. "And I expect, even if Mama and Daddy didn't squash your creativity, Aunt Cecelia would have plenty to say about any ideas that were too wild."

"Yes." Becca sighed. After a moment,

her face brightened. "But then, Aunt Cecelia's getting married."

"And it's time to meet Aunt Cecelia," I said.

We did. We got there early. Of course, Aunt Cecelia was there early, too. She was holding a shopping bag, but I couldn't tell what was in it.

"I need a little more time." Aunt Cecelia eyed us. "You can come with me if you'd like or . . ."

"Let's just meet back here in another hour," I suggested quickly.

Did Aunt Cecelia look relieved? Did she have more wedding shopping to do? We certainly did!

"Very well," she said.

We coordinated watches again, and set off. Becca and I almost shopped until we dropped. We went to Steven E's, we went to Laura Ashley, we went to shops on all five levels of Washington Mall, including Rita's Bridal Shoppe (silk suits in pastel colours are very popular for second or "post-first marriage" ceremonies, in case you wanted to know).

Even with a stop at Donut Delite for some sugar reinforcements, I was more than ready to go and meet Aunt Cecelia.

"Phew!" I gasped, falling into the front seat of the car.

"Tired?" asked Aunt Cecelia.

"Hmm," I said.

Becca flopped down in the back seat. She was too tired even to make a sound. I closed my eyes for *just* a minute and the next thing I knew, Aunt Cecelia was going, "Girls, we're home."

Wow! I'd fallen asleep!

Becca and I got sleepily out of the car and offered to help Aunt Cecelia with her bags.

"I've got them," she said. Which of course meant we couldn't find out what was in them.

"Did you find everything you were shopping for?" I asked, waking up a little.

"Go on into the house. It's too cold to be standing around chatting."

Aunt Cecelia gave me a little push and Becca and I turned and went obediently into the house. I turned to close the front door and stopped and grabbed Becca's arm dramatically. "Look! It's *his* car!"

Without even thinking about it I closed the door and dragged Becca over to the front window.

"Cece, I was just driving by. Let me help you with those," Mr Major said, getting out of his car.

"I suppose you could," said Cece. She smiled at Mr Major and for some reason they both laughed. Then Aunt Cecelia said, "But you can't stay. I've got work to do."

"Well, Cece, that's fine," said Mr Major.

I wrinkled my nose at Becca. That wasn't very romantic of Aunt Cecelia. And besides, what about having love to keep her warm, the way the songs all said?

"Don't forget, Saturday at four o'clock," said Aunt Cecelia.

Mr Major reached into his pocket and pulled out his diary. He flipped it open and read out a time and date. "Written in ink," he assured Aunt Cecelia. "I'll be there. Will you?"

A little more romantic. I suppose.

"You know I will," said Aunt Cecelia. "Now go before you freeze to death." She went inside and shut the door.

Mr Major was shaking his head and laughing as he walked back to the car. We listened as Aunt Cecelia carried her shopping bags to her room.

Becca looked at me, her eyes shining. "That's it," she said. "That's when Aunt Cecelia's wedding is!"

We high fived and then ran into the kitchen.

8th
CHAPTER

Saturday

Okay. Danielle's a great kid. A tough kid. A brave kid. But she's also a kid who needs to rein it in a little. I mean, even though I was prepared for her "high spirits" by what you guys had told me, I wasn't prepared enough....

Weddings seemed to be a theme these days. When Kristy arrived at the Robertses' on Saturday afternoon, they were all dressed up to go to the wedding of a friend of Mr Roberts.

Mrs Roberts was just pulling on her coat while Mr Roberts was warming up the car.

"The wedding present ... ah, here it is. Good. You're right on time, Kristy. That's great. We'll be back about five-thirty, I think. We'll just drop in at the reception, but we're not going to stay long. Phone numbers where we can be reached are by the phone in the kitchen. Also, doctors' numbers and any other numbers you might need."

"Great," Kristy said approvingly.

"The bad news is that Greg has a cold. He's in his room and I want him to stay in bed. He needs to be kept quiet, but he doesn't necessarily have to sleep. I just don't want his cold to turn into anything worse in this weather. And I'd like to prevent Danielle from getting it." Mrs Roberts paused and smiled a little. "Although I don't think a cold would slow Danielle down a bit. She's doing so well, Kristy."

Kristy nodded.

Mrs Roberts became brisk and practical

again. "Danielle asked if she could invite some friends over and I said okay. I imagine that's where she is right now, on the phone. That's a lot of kids for you to keep an eye on so our neighbours, the Isaacs, are on call if you need help. Greg doesn't need any medicine; I've just given him some. But all the juice and liquid he wants. And snacks for Danielle and her friends are fine later on, too. There's even some frozen dough in the freezer if you want to make biscuits."

"Got it," Kristy said. "Have a good time at the wedding."

"Thanks," said Mrs Roberts, and then she was gone.

Sure enough, Danielle was on the phone when Kristy put her head round the playroom door. Danielle waved at her and made elaborate hand motions which Kristy took to mean that she was on the phone and would be getting off in just a minute. Kristy pointed down the hall and made a sneezing motion and Danielle grinned widely.

What everyone had been saying was true. Danielle did look great. A little thin, but full of life and energy.

Greg didn't look so great. In fact, he looked cranky and miserable.

"Hi, Greg," Kristy said. "I'm Kristy."

"I doe," he said through his stuffed nose. He frowned. "Cad I have a Coke?"

"You can have some juice."

He frowned again.

"I'll get you some and be right back," Kristy said, taking this as not exactly a no, and she picked up his glass from the table by the bed and went back to the kitchen. She filled the glass about two-thirds full with orange juice, then added some soda water. It was healthier than a Coke (she could almost hear Dawn giving it the Dawn seal of approval), but it had some fizz.

On the way back to Greg's room, she ran into Danielle, who'd just come bouncing out in the hall.

"Hi, Kristy!"

"Hi, yourself. You've got company coming?"

Danielle grinned her great grin. "Becca, Charlotte, *and* Vanessa!"

"That's not just friends, that's a party!"

"Yes. I better go and tidy up my room a bit before they get here."

Kristy took that as a good sign. "Go for it," she said. "I'm in with Greg right now. I'll check back with you in a little while."

"Check!" said Danielle, giggling, and she bounced away.

Kristy took the juice into Greg. "Kristy's special orange soda," she said.

Greg looked a little less cranky at this. He sat up and took a small, suspicious sip of the juice. He wrinkled his nose. "It's not real orange soda."

"It is," said Kristy. "The real-est. Made from real orange juice."

Greg took another sip. Then he took several noisy gulps. "It's pretty good," he said, putting the glass to one side.

"I hear you've already had your medicine," said Kristy.

With an awful face, Greg said, "It's disgusting."

"Yes," said Kristy sympathetically. "But at least you don't have to have any more for a while. Maybe we could do something fun for a little while. Like read or—"

"Play cards!" said Greg.

That caught Kristy by surprise. But it was a quiet activity (as long as they didn't play slap jack or fifty-two pick up), so she settled down for some marathon card playing.

The "party" arrived not long after that, Becca and Charlotte first, then Haley Braddock, then Vanessa Pike, one of Mallory's younger sisters.

"It's snowing, I'm glowing," said Vanessa, coming in the door. Kristy peered out past her and saw a few flakes.

Enough, anyway, for Vanessa-the-poet to make a rhyme.

"We've got some dough for making biscuits later," she said to the girls who were now gathered in the hall while Vanessa took off her coat. "Maybe we can make some hot chocolate then, too."

"I like hot chocolate," said Becca.

"Or hot jelly," said Haley.

"Hot jelly?" asked Kristy.

"You know," Haley said. "You make jelly but instead of putting it into the fridge you drink it."

The thought of all that sugar made Kristy's teeth ache. It was junk food worthy of Claudia. But she just nodded and said, "We'll see."

"Come on, you lot," said Danielle.

"Don't forget Greg's not feeling well," Kristy reminded them. "So keep it sort of quiet, okay?"

"Don't worry," said Danielle. "I know how that feels!"

True, thought Kristy, as she headed back to Greg's room. Maybe Danielle was getting over her "high spirits".

When she went back into Greg's room, he was turning restlessly. Some of the cards had fallen off the bed. "My head hurts," he complained.

Gathering up the cards, Kristy said,

"Why don't I just read to you for a little while? Would you like that?"

"I suppose so," said Greg.

She felt his forehead, but it didn't seem warm. But maybe playing cards while he had a cold *had* made his head hurt. His eyes looked a little heavy, too. Maybe reading to him would settle him down and he could sleep until his headache went away.

"Any book you want," she said. "You name it."

As it turned out, he couldn't make up his mind, and she spent the next half hour or so book-surfing: reading a few lines or paragraphs from one book, only to have Greg say fretfully, "Not that one."

Meanwhile, Danielle and her friends had come up with a fairly spectacular way to entertain themselves.

They'd decided to build a swimming pool—in the Robertses' bathroom.

It *was* a quiet activity. But Danielle must have known it wasn't on the list of things a babysitter could allow. Or parents either.

It started with the sound of the water running. Kristy wouldn't have even noticed it, except that the water kept running. And running. She thought maybe someone had forgotten to turn off a tap.

She looked at Greg. His eyes were drooping. She shut the book and waited a moment and when he didn't wake up she slipped out of the room to check on things.

No water running in the kitchen. She went down the hall to the bathroom. No water there.

Kristy frowned.

Then she thought, maybe there's another bathroom. She walked down the hall, past Danielle's room and stopped outside a door at the end of the hall.

The door was closed. Kristy pushed it open. In the Robertses' bedroom, everything looked normal. But she could hear the sound of running water much more clearly now. A shower of water.

The sound was coming from behind the closed door across the room. Still calm (like a good babysitter should be), she walked quickly across the room and opened the door.

Five startled faces turned towards her.

"Uh-oh!" said Charlotte. She made a grab for the shower door, the sliding glass kind that sits on the top edge of the bath. It was closed. When Charlotte grabbed it, it came open.

A flood of incredible-coloured water

poured out across the bathroom floor—and Kristy's feet.

"Kristy!" gasped Haley.

Danielle didn't say anything. She made a leap for the shower door and closed it. But it was too late.

The girls and Kristy were standing in the middle of a blue-green-yellow-red-orange lake.

"*What* is going on?" cried Kristy. She realized that the sea of water was spreading into the bedroom and made a dive for the door connecting the bathroom to the bedroom. She closed it. But it was too late. The water had already spilled out into the bedroom.

"We wanted to see if we could fill the shower up all the way to the top," said Danielle, as if it were the most obvious thing in the world.

"We used Easter egg dye to make it pretty colours," added Haley.

"Only we didn't have enough dye," said Becca.

Sure enough, the girls had put the plug in the bath, turned on the shower, and *taped* up all the places where water might have leaked out around the shower door. And the shower was still running.

"How were you going to get the door open and turn the water off once the shower was full?" asked Kristy in exasperation. "Climb over the top and dive?"

No one answered. Kristy realized that she had just guessed part two of the plan to build an indoor swimming pool in the bathroom. "Good grief!" she said. "You can't . . ." Her voice trailed off. She remembered the discussion that we'd had at the BSC meeting about Danielle, and decided not to talk to her about this "overabundance" of high spirits. She just couldn't do it.

Besides, maybe it would be better to talk to the Robertses when they got home.

"Are you going to tell?" asked Danielle.

"Well," said Kristy slowly. "Maybe, maybe not," she said again. "But don't do that again, okay?"

"Okay," said Danielle. If Kristy had been watching closely, she might have seen the mischief in Danielle's eyes. But it had been a long afternoon. She also didn't quite catch the significance when Danielle exchanged a look with Charlotte, Vanessa, Becca and Haley, and said, solemnly, "I promise. I'll never do *that* again."

Kristy took a deep breath. Then she said, "Never mind. We need to get this mess cleaned up. Now."

She opened the shower door (fortunately, the shower hadn't had a chance to fill up much), turned the water off and took out the bath plug.

"Haley, you and Char peel this tape off and get the sticky stuff off, too, and throw it all away. Danielle, go and get a mop and a bucket and some paper towels. All of you, take off your shoes and socks and trousers. Vanessa, you're in charge of washing and drying all the clothes."

It was a mess. A huge mess. Everything in the bathroom was completely soaked, and dyed—including the towels hanging on the wall and the toilet paper.

But with Kristy in charge, the bathroom was soon dry, the toilet paper changed, the towels in the laundry and fresh towels put out, and five girls restored to more or less their normal appearance. The carpet in the bedroom around the bathroom door (which fortunately was dark blue so it didn't show the effects of the Easter egg dye) was still a little damp to the touch, but Kristy decided that it would dry out pretty quickly.

She had a quick look at Greg, who was asleep on his back with his mouth open, and herded the gang of five into the kitchen for hot chocolate. Which is where they were all sitting when the Robertses returned. It was a heart-warming scene that met Mrs Roberts' eyes when she came into the kitchen, and she didn't notice Vanessa's rainbow socks, or the funny high-tide mark around the calves of Becca's jeans.

"Mum!" Danielle jumped up and gave her mother an exuberant hug. "How was the wedding?"

"Beautiful, just the way weddings are supposed to be," answered Mrs Roberts with a smile.

She went into the hall to hang up her coat and Kristy followed her, wondering if she should tell her what had happened after all. But Mrs Roberts cut her off. "Thanks for taking such good care of things, Kristy."

"No problem. But I—"

"You know, seeing Danielle like this, I can't even let myself worry that her next doctor's appointment is coming up."

"Doctor's appointment?" Kristy heard her own voice go up with worry.

Mrs Roberts heard it, too. She made a little face and patted Kristy on the shoulder. "Just routine. All the signs are that Danielle's health is stable, if not improving. That she's still in remission. Don't worry."

How could Kristy tell Mrs Roberts about the great bathroom swimming pool flood? She couldn't. Not with another doctor's appointment staring Danielle—and the Robertses—in the face.

So she left without saying anything at all.

That night, Kristy phoned Mary Anne and me about what had happened, as we'd been there for the other "high-spirited" incidents.

"I don't know," Kristy said to me. "I just don't know. I mean, Mary Anne thinks it's time one of us had a talk with Mrs Roberts. What do you think?"

"You're asking me?" I said. I'm not used to even a speck of indecision in Kristy. But then, this was a special case.

I thought hard. Finally I said slowly, "I agree with Mary Anne. Danielle has got too—creative—an imagination for us to let this go on. You know, she's acting kind of, well, spoiled. Not in a nasty way, but in a way that says she knows she can get away with things."

I wasn't sure I had made myself clear, but Kristy seemed to understand. "You're right," she said. "One of us needs to talk to Mrs Roberts. Let me think about this and we'll talk it over on Monday at our meeting."

"Good," I said. And I meant it.

# 9th CHAPTER

"This meeting of the Babysitters Club will—" Kristy stopped.

Stacey walked in the door.

Kristy looked at her watch.

Stacey sat down, reached into her rucksack, and pulled out a bag of pretzels. She opened it and offered it to Dawn.

Kristy cleared her throat. "Thanks for coming to the meeting, Stacey."

Looking up, Stacey said, "Oh. Am I late? Gosh, I am sorry!" She began to munch on a pretzel. And she didn't sound terribly sorry. At least not sorry enough for Kristy. Kristy gave her a Look, cleared her throat again, and said, "This meeting of the BSC will *now* come to order. Feel free to collect subs whenever you like, Stacey." (Monday is subs day.)

"Oh, right," said Stacey. Mary Anne handed her the record book and we began to fork our subs over to her.

"So what about Danielle?" I asked quickly.

"Right, Danielle," said Kristy. She paused. "I haven't quite decided what to do." She filled the rest of us in on what had happened.

"Amazing!" said Dawn. "Danielle's an amazing kid."

'Yes," said Kristy. "Maybe too amazing for her own good. Who knows what she'll think of next?"

"She keeps pushing the boundaries," said Mary Anne. "Seeing what she can get away with. You can't blame her. I mean, it's probably a long time since she felt like a kid."

"Yes, but she's going to go too far. And then what's going to happen?" argued Dawn.

I said, "Kristy, why don't you phone Mrs Roberts now? With all of us here. You can tell her what happened. And I can talk to her as well, if you need it."

"Me, too," said Mary Anne. "It might carry more weight coming from all of us."

"And there's nothing wrong with a little support when you're telling a parent that her child might be just a tiny bit out of control," said Kristy with a wry grin. "Okay."

Mary Anne gave Kristy the number from the client list and Kristy rang the Robertses.

"Mrs Roberts? Hi. It's Kristy Thomas, from the Babysitters Club... Yes. Fine, thank you. How are you?... Good. And Danielle?... I'm glad. Actually, it's about Danielle I'm calling... No, no, nothing major. Not exactly. Well, it's about this past Saturday afternoon."

Trying to sound very adult and neutral, Kristy told Mrs Roberts about the bathtub-swimming pool idea.

She listened for a moment when she finished, frowned, and said, "But that's not all. Both Mary Anne Spier and Jessi had some problems, too."

Kristy told Mrs Roberts about the Rollerblading incident and the mattress-toboggan-run in the basement.

A look of surprise came over her face. "Really?" she said. "Are you sure? No! No, of course not. It's just that ... I see. Well, of course. We're all glad she feels so much better. We just felt that we had to let you know. Right. You're welcome."

Slowly hanging up the phone, Kristy said, "She didn't think it was serious. Any of it. She said it's just high spirits and

Danielle will work them off and settle down to 'medium speed'. That's it."

"It's more than that!" I couldn't help exclaiming. "Do you want me to call her back?"

Kristy shook her head. "No. I mean, she *is* Danielle's mother. She knows Danielle better than we do. She's the best judge of how to handle this. And maybe she is right."

No one said anything to that. Then Mary Anne said, "Well, you've done all you can do."

"True," said Kristy. But she didn't look happy. And I admit, I wasn't too happy about it, either.

The phone started ringing and we arranged a couple of babysitting jobs, and by then, I had remembered something that did make me happy.

Aunt Cecelia's wedding.

It was still a secret in our family. A big secret. I decided that it was just like Aunt Cecelia not to want a fuss over it all. She'd probably have a tiny wedding, just family. But I also knew how important it was for us to look just right for Aunt Cecelia's wedding, and Becca and I had Made Plans.

After all, we knew the date—this coming Saturday. And we were prepared.

We hadn't been able to come up with the money for new clothes *and* an expensive wedding gift. So we'd settled on a small gift (a book of passes to the Stoneybrook Cinema).

Everyone approved of that idea, even Kristy-the-great-idea person. "I bet that's something neither your aunt or her new husband has!" she said.

"So, are we invited, or what?" asked Claudia. "I've got a cool idea for my dress."

"Sorry," I said. "I wish you could be there. But I'm sure this is going to be a super-small wedding. I mean, it's so super-secret already."

"A secret wedding," said Mary Anne, her eyes misting over. "That's *so* romantic."

Romantic is not a word I'd use in association with my aunt Cecelia. I had a feeling the small, secret nature of the wedding had more to do with practicality than romance. But I didn't say anything to spoil it for Mary Anne. Besides, any wedding, even Aunt Cecelia's, has romance built into it, right?

We talked about weddings—Aunt Cecelia's, Dawn's father's, Dawn's mother's and Mary Anne's father's, Kristy's mum's—and even the wedding that the Robertses had gone to on Saturday until the meeting was over. Stacey reminded us that in New York, some brides even wore black, but I was sure Aunt Cecelia would be going for a silk suit or some tailored dress.

"Do you think she'll promise to obey?" asked Mal, giggling.

"Not Aunt Cecelia!" I shot back.

Kristy looked at her watch. "Okay, you wedding fiends, listen. This meeting of the BSC is officially adjourned."

"Here comes the briide," sang Claudia, way, *way* off-key.

I shook my head and jumped up. We went downstairs, and as Mal and I went out of the door, I heard Claudia shout, "Take lots of pictures."

"Maybe the BSC could buy a present, too," I heard Kristy add. "You know, from one group of babysitters to another babysitter."

Mal and I exchanged glances, remembering when Aunt Cecelia had tried to be my babysitter. Good thing we'd worked that out.

Laughing, we headed for home—and the wedding week countdown.

# 10th CHAPTER

"Here comes the bride," I hummed. Softly. It was early Saturday morning. The big day.

I looked under my eyelashes at my mum, who had propped her chin on her hand, and was reading the newspaper and drinking hot tea. She didn't even look awake.

My parents were keeping the wedding a secret right up till the end. And they were doing a very good job of not even letting on that they knew.

But then so were Becca and I. My parents and Aunt Cecelia thought they were going to give us a big surprise. But Becca and I (and Squirt) were going to give them a big surprise, too.

My father came down for breakfast just as I finished. I hummed a few more bars of "The Wedding March", but he didn't react, either. He just started making toast.

"Aunt Cecelia's not up yet, is she?" I asked casually.

My father looked up. "Not yet, I suppose," he answered, just as casually.

"Well, see you lot later," I said.

"Mmm," said my mum, turning a page of the newspaper.

"Mmmm," said my father, buttering the toast.

Becca was sitting on the floor of her room with the wrapping paper, tape and scissors by her. The Stoneybrook Cinema coupon book was on her lap.

"It's so little," she said, looking up when I came in. "It's rather hard to wrap."

She was right—it was hard. When we were finished, it looked, well, wrapped. Not exactly a professional wrapping job. "It's the thought that counts," I announced. "And big things come in small packages. Besides, we're going to have to hurry to get ready. Don't forget, the wedding is at eleven. We need to get downstairs early so they don't leave and get married without us!"

Becca made a mad dash for the shower while I scooped Squirt up and put him in his best winter outfit: a white polo-neck shirt and a little navy jacket that buttoned up the front, with a pair of matching navy elastic-waisted baby trousers.

Then I made a dash for the shower while Becca kept an eye on Squirt to make sure he didn't mess up his super-cool baby look.

We hadn't been able to buy new dresses, but we'd got new tights to go with our old dresses, and we'd bought matching ribbons, too, to braid into our hair. We took turns braiding each other's hair (with Squirt taking an *extreme* interest in the ribbons).

At last we were ready. I picked up Squirt, and Becca picked up the present, and we checked ourselves in the mirror. We looked great. We'd do Aunt Cecelia— or anybody, for that matter—proud.

It was ten-thirty sharp.

"I hear a car pulling into the drive," Becca said with a gasp.

We hurried out of the room and down the stairs as the doorbell rang. We reached the living room just as Aunt Cecelia ushered Mr Major in.

"Da, da, da, *da*!" I sang as we walked in.

"Jessica? Rebecca? John Philip?" said Aunt Cecelia in complete surprise.

"Surprise!" Becca and I answered together.

"AAAhee," chimed in Squirt, waving his arms happily.

"What's going on?" asked Mama, coming into the room with the newspaper in her hand. She was wearing leggings and a big old sweater. Daddy followed her, holding a cup of coffee. He had on a pair of old jeans and his college sweatshirt.

"But—you're not even dressed yet!" I cried in horror.

"Dressed for what?" asked Daddy.

I looked at Mama and Daddy. I looked at Aunt Cecelia and Mr Major. Mr Major was wearing a suit. A nice suit. But it didn't say wedding. And Aunt Cecelia was wearing a nice suit, too. One she called "Old Reliable" because she could wear it almost anywhere and it looked right.

I looked down at me, dressed to the nines. I looked at Squirt. My eyes met Becca's.

"The—the wedding?" I asked.

"What wedding?" said Mama. "Not the one Cecelia and Martin are going to be in?"

"Be in? Be in how?" I was getting a bad feeling about this. A really bad feeling.

"Well, Mr Major is an usher," said

Aunt Cecelia. "And I'm in charge of the guest book."

"That's it? You're going to *someone else's* wedding?" asked Becca. "But we thought—aren't you and Mr Major getting married?"

"Married!"

Aunt Cecelia and Mr Major exchanged glances and they both burst out laughing.

"You're not getting married?" I asked, just to make sure.

"No," said Aunt Cecelia, still laughing.

Mr Major shook his head.

"Where on earth did you get an idea like that?" asked Mama.

"Er, well . . . I suppose we saw you together and sort of jumped to conclusions," I said.

"And heard me and Mr Major talking about this wedding at some point," Aunt Cecelia guessed shrewdly.

I nodded. I was mortified.

"Sorry to disappoint you girls," said Mr Major. His face was amused, but his smile was a kind one. "I wish we could take you to the wedding. You look very nice."

"Thanks," said Becca. "Er, have a good time."

"We will," said Aunt Cecelia. She shook her head, and she and Mr Major left.

"I suppose we'd better get out of our good clothes," I said quickly, before Mama or Daddy could say anything else. We beat a hasty retreat up the stairs. We heard them laughing as we reached the top.

"I don't believe it," said Becca. "I just don't believe it!"

"Me, neither," I said dejectedly. "We'll probably never hear the end of this. You know how adults get sometimes."

"At least we can use these cinema passes ourselves," she said.

The thought didn't cheer me up very much. And I felt even less cheerful when I realized something else.

All my friends, everyone in the BSC, thought Aunt Cecelia was getting married. They thought I was spending Saturday at a wedding. They were expecting pictures, stories, photographs. They were even talking about buying them a present.

Total mortification. I could imagine Kristy's reaction. And Claudia's. And everybody's. Not that they'd be nasty or anything. But they'd laugh in spite of themselves. At the very least.

What was I going to tell them? What was I going to do now?

# 11th CHAPTER

I had just got out of my wedding dress (and deeper into the wedding bell blues) when the phone rang.

It was Stacey.

"Oh, Jessi, I'm glad you're at home," she said breathlessly. (Normally I would have been annoyed that she'd already forgotten I was supposed to spend Saturday at a wedding. But now I was glad. I certainly wasn't going to bring it up.)

"Hi," I said noncommittally. If she'd forgotten about the wedding, I didn't want to remind her.

She really had forgotten. "Listen, I'm supposed to sit for Danielle and Greg Roberts in half an hour. But I can't. Something's come up. So could you do it for me?"

"Half an hour?" I checked my watch. It was eleven-thirty.

"I know it's short notice. I'm really sorry."

It was short notice. And that was a little annoying. But the job would get me out of the house and away from my family (and Aunt Cecelia and Mr Major when they got back). And it would take my mind off my wedding bell blues.

"I can do it," I said.

"You're the best," said Stacey. "I'll ring Mrs Roberts and let her know you're on the way." And she rang off.

When I told Becca where I was going, I could tell she felt the same way: a chance to get out of the house before we could hear any wedding humour at our expense. "Can I phone Danielle and ask if I can come, too?" she asked.

"Of course," I said. "If it's okay with Mama."

It was, of course, and a few minutes later Becca and I were on our way to the Robertses'. "Danielle's called Char and Vanessa and Haley, too," she said.

"Great," I replied. At least Becca didn't seem too embarrassed about what had happened. Or she was recovering faster than I was.

When we reached the Robertses', Mrs

Roberts answered the door, laughing and shaking her head. "Hi, Becca. The others beat you here. They're in the playroom."

"Hi, Mrs Roberts." Becca shot down the hall, struggling out of her coat as she ran.

"It's total chaos here today, Jessi. I hope you have nerves of steel!" Mrs Roberts said.

I can't say I really liked the sound of that. But I was still thinking about the wedding that wasn't. I nodded and concentrated on what Mrs Roberts was saying about when she'd be back, and what was happening, and that I could call Mrs Isaacs over if I needed a hand with the kids.

"Greg's got over his cold," Mrs Roberts concluded. "But he's still a little under the weather. If Mr Roberts calls, please tell him not to worry. I haven't forgotten that he doesn't have his car and I will pick him up."

I nodded and waved goodbye to Mrs Roberts as she left. She wouldn't be back till late in the afternoon, so I had a long job ahead of me. I was glad of that.

I found the fearsome fivesome engaged in some complicated game of Pictionary in the playroom. That was a relief. I knew that would keep them busy a long time.

Greg and I settled down for a game of draughts in his room. (I confess, I love draughts. I always have.)

"We've finished playing Pictionary," a voice announced from the door. I looked up to see the five girls standing in the doorway. Danielle went on, "We're going to play 'Let's Go on a Car Trip' now."

"How do you play that?" I asked, pleased that Danielle was keeping me informed about her activities. Maybe the swimming pool/shower disaster had taught her a lesson after all.

"You pack a suitcase and plan a trip. And you make a picnic lunch. Can we make our lunches and pretend they're picnic lunches?"

I had to grin at that. Trust an optimist like Danielle to come up with a new way to have a picnic lunch in the middle of winter.

"Okay," I said. "Just leave some for Greg and me when we get ready for lunch."

Greg and I played draughts and the five girls played "Going on a Trip" and peace reigned. When Greg and I went downstairs to make lunch, the kitchen was spotless. We took our lunches back to Greg's room for a picnic of our own and began a draughts world record marathon.

Not too long after that, I heard Danielle say from the hallway, "Let's go out to the garage now."

I smiled to myself, glad it wasn't too cold for them to keep playing their game. Then I triple-jumped Greg.

Twenty minutes later, I decided to check on Danielle and her trip-mates.

I opened the kitchen door. They weren't in the garage.

Neither was the car.

Trying not to believe the worst, I walked quickly to the open garage door. The car wasn't in the drive. It wasn't parked out the front, either.

Then I saw it. It was coming at a snail's pace down the road from the cul-de-sac at the end of the street. As it turned erratically into the drive, I could just see Danielle's triumphant face half hidden behind the wheel.

My mouth dropped open. I couldn't believe my eyes.

Neither could Danielle. Her eyes widened in panic. The car lurched forward towards me. I jumped sideways and stumbled.

The car stopped.

Relief washed over me. But it was too soon. As I got up, my hands shaking, the car began to roll backwards down the drive.

"Nooooo!" I screamed. "The brakes. The brakes, Danielle, the brakes. Put on the braaaaakes!"

But it was no use. I was screaming and running in slow motion. I'd never reach the car in time.

The car rolled back out of the drive and into the street. It smashed into another car parked across the street.

For one awful moment I froze. Then I ran forward again towards the wreck.

# 12th CHAPTER

I don't remember running down the drive. The next thing I knew, I was wrenching open the door of the car.

Charlotte and Haley were screaming. Becca had started to cry. Vanessa, who'd been sitting next to Danielle, was holding her hand up to her forehead, her expression dazed.

Danielle was perfectly white, her eyes huge in her thin face.

"Are you all right?"

Danielle nodded slightly. I turned towards Charlotte and Haley and said, *"Don't scream. Stop it. Now!"*

They stopped. "Becca, it's okay. Charlotte, Haley, Becca, Danielle, out of the car," I ordered.

Some other part of me had taken over. I was responsible. I had to act responsible.

I could have the hysterics I felt threatening to overwhelm me later.

Vanessa sat without moving, her hand against her head. Fighting down the fear I felt, I helped the others out of the car. "Stay right there," I ordered, pointing to the pavement. "Don't move!"

A man's voice beside me said, "I was washing up and saw the whole thing from my kitchen window. I've called the police."

"I think Vanessa's hurt," I said. "Vanessa, can you hear me? It's Jessi."

She looked at me. At last she said, "Jessi, my head hurts."

"I'll call the ambulance," the man said and was gone. As he left, I heard him say to the crowd that had begun to form, "There's been a slight accident. The police are on their way. Please stand back."

Then I heard Danielle say, "I'm sorry about your car, Mrs Isaacs."

"Cars can be repaired," said a woman's voice. "Why don't you children come inside with me?"

"Jessi said we had to stay right here." My little sister's voice.

"Don't move," I told Vanessa. I could see blood coming from between her fingers. Had her head hit the windscreen? How hard?

Sirens wailed.

Mrs Isaacs swam into view. I was relieved to see she looked calm, not angry. "Jessi? I'm Mrs Isaacs. I'm going to go and phone the Robertses now, and then take the girls and Greg into my house. Mr Isaacs will be out to help you with the police."

"Thank you," I said gratefully.

The police and the ambulance arrived at the same time. I don't remember much of what happened next, just that I kept saying, "Vanessa can't go to the hospital by herself. I'm responsible."

I couldn't ride in the ambulance, so the police took me in the patrol car, their sirens wailing. I did remember to give Mr Isaacs the phone numbers for my parents and Charlotte's and Haley's and Vanessa's. I got Mr Isaacs' phone number, too.

Then I was in the Casualty waiting room at the hospital, holding Vanessa's hand for a moment as she lay on a stretcher. A few minutes later Mrs Pike arrived.

I've never been so glad to see somebody in my life.

Another long blank period of time passed and then my father was bending over me saying, "Jessi. It's me. Daddy."

And I threw myself in my father's arms and began to cry.

When I got home, Aunt Cecelia put me straight to bed (Mama was on her way home from the shop). Normally, I would have resented Aunt Cecelia's bossiness. But this time I was grateful for it, grateful not to be the one responsible. Grateful not to be the one in charge.

And I was suddenly sooo tired. "I've got to phone the Robertses," I protested weakly.

"I've already talked to them. And the Pikes. And Johanssens. And the Braddocks," Aunt Cecelia told me. "You can talk to them later. I've already put Becca to bed. Now do what I say."

I was too exhausted to argue. I opened my mouth to say something. And I fell asleep.

When I woke up it wasn't much later, but I felt as if I'd been asleep for hours. I got up. I ached, too, as if I'd been the one in the car crash.

I went slowly downstairs. Mama and Daddy and Aunt Cecelia were sitting at the kitchen table.

"Hi," I said.

Mama jumped up and put her hand on my forehead as if I was a little kid.

"I'm okay," I told her.

"I hear you were more than okay," said Mama. She smoothed my hair back. "I hear you were very responsible today."

"She was," said my aunt.

I smiled a little at that. I must have done all right if strict Aunt Cecelia said so. It made me feel a little better.

Daddy said, "Your friends have all been phoning. You might want to ring them back."

"The Robertses first," I said. Then I gasped, "Mal! Vanessa! Is Vanessa—?"

"Mal called to tell you not to worry. It was a small cut. They put a stitch in it at Casualty. She must have bumped her head against the front windscreen somehow. But she doesn't have concussion."

It was too scary to think about. I pushed away the image of Vanessa sitting there in shock, her hand against her head.

"Will you excuse me?" I said. "I've got to make a phone call."

Mrs Roberts answered on the first ring. "Jessi," she said. "I'm so sorry all this happened! Are you okay?"

"I'm fine," I said. "A little shaken up, but otherwise just fine. How's Danielle?"

"She's fine, too," said Mrs Roberts. "Could you hold a minute?" I heard her calling Mr Roberts and a few minutes later he got on the extension.

112

"We both want to apologize," said Mr Roberts. "We've been a little too indulgent—no, much too indulgent—of Danielle lately. We just refused to see that we were spoiling her, letting her get away with things we wouldn't have otherwise allowed if she hadn't been ill."

"Yes," said Mrs Roberts. "She's been so ill ... but it wasn't fair to her or to Greg or to you or to any of us to let her keep testing our limits like that. We should have called a stop to it at the beginning. You and your friends tried to warn us and we just wouldn't listen."

Relief washed over me. "Thank you," I said. "I mean, I'm glad ..."

"Don't thank us," said Mr Roberts. "Things will be a little different from now on. Danielle will be free to enjoy high spirits just like any other kid. But she won't be allowed to abuse that privilege."

I hung up feeling much, much better.

Then I called Mal. Vanessa was doing fine, Mal told me, and rather proud of her stitch. It was her first.

We both laughed at that. Then I told her about the conversation with the Robertses.

"I'm so glad," said Mal. "I know everybody else will be, too."

"Yes," I said. I yawned hugely. Maybe I'd go to bed early.

But I didn't go to bed straight away. I made about a million more phone calls—to the Braddocks and the Johanssens (both of whom assured me that Haley and Charlotte, respectively, were just fine and in a lot of trouble) and to the other members of the BSC.

Everyone I talked to agreed with the Robertses—that what had happened wasn't my fault. And every member of the BSC was also in agreement. We had been treating Danielle differently because she'd been ill. And that really wasn't fair on anyone, including Danielle.

# 13th CHAPTER

Monday

Danielle's great ideas seem to have lost their popularity with her friends. In fact, Danielle seems to have lost her friends. All of them. I think she drove herself into even bigger trouble than we realized...

A whole week and two days had passed since Danielle's trip game turned out so badly. She'd been the topic of much conversation at the BSC meetings. In fact, she and her exploits had been just about the only topic of conversation. I'd talked to the Robertses once since the accident, just to make sure Danielle was doing all right (she was, and, in addition, had been to the doctor's, who'd said she was still in remission and still thriving).

We were all cheered by that good news. But Stacey still didn't know what to expect when she arrived for her babysitting job nine days later.

Whatever she expected, it wasn't what she found.

Greg was busy writing a report for school the next day. His topic was fire engines and as he was only in first grade, it involved a lot of illustration. Stacey left him at his desk amid a pile of red crayons and pencils, promising she'd be back to check on him from time to time—and to call him for a snack a little later on.

She went to find Danielle. She didn't have far to go. Danielle was dialling a number on the phone in the playroom. As she spoke into the receiver, Stacey stopped in the doorway.

"Hello, Vanessa? How are—? Vanessa? Vanessa? Awwww . . ."

She hung up the phone hard, and dialled it again almost immediately. "Hello, this is Danielle. Is Haley there? She *is*? At Vanessa's? Thank you. No. 'Bye."

She hung up the phone again and her thin shoulders slumped.

Stacey cleared her throat. "Hi, Danielle. It's me. Stacey."

"Hi, Stacey," said Danielle listlessly. She turned and stared at Stacey. Well, not exactly at Stacey. She couldn't quite meet her eye. She stared at Stacey's left ear. "You heard what I did?"

Best to meet this head on, thought Stacey. "Yes," she said.

Danielle frowned. She turned and picked up the phone again. This time, while Stacey listened, Danielle called Becca.

"Becca? I just wanted to—Charlotte's there, too? Well, could I—? Becca? Becca?"

My little sister had hung up on Danielle, too. But not before making it clear that Charlotte was also there, and they were *both* hanging up on Danielle.

Danielle hung up the phone.

"I suppose your friends are pretty angry with you," said Stacey.

Danielle nodded. Tears welled in her eyes. She blinked rapidly to keep them back.

That was unexpected, too. Stacey knew how tough and upbeat Danielle was. She didn't think anybody had ever seen Danielle cry.

Or even almost cry.

Danielle turned back to the phone and punched in another number. She said. "Hello. Listen, Vanessa . . ." She stopped. She hung up.

Turning her back to the telephone, Danielle slid down until she was sitting upright on the floor against the wall in the corner next to the phone, her knees drawn up, her arms wrapped tightly around her legs. "I know what I did was wrong," she said. "I know it was really dangerous. And stupid. I know I should have thought about what I was doing. I'm sorry. I told them I was sorry. I even wrote them notes. But none of them will speak to me!"

The last words ended in a kind of wail.

Stacey sat down cross-legged, facing Danielle. "Sometimes it takes time for people to get over being angry or upset," said Stacey. "Maybe you should give your friends more time."

She looked at Danielle's pinched face. She heard the word "time". Who was she to talk to a kid like Danielle about time? Okay, so we'd all decided not to indulge her just because she was ill. But Stacey couldn't take this.

"Excuse me," said Stacey. She leaned across Danielle and grabbed the phone. She dialled two familiar numbers: mine and Mal's.

"What are you doing?" asked Danielle, who'd been listening to Stacey's requests to Mal and me wide-eyed.

"Trust me. This is a job for the BSC," Stacey said, trying to keep her tone light.

"Can Mal and Jessi really do that? What you asked them to?"

"Yes. And they will, too." Stacey looked at her watch. "I'd give them about twenty minutes, okay?"

Twenty minutes later, almost exactly, the doorbell rang.

I stood there, with Becca and Charlotte in tow. Neither of them was happy about it. Neither, from the looks of things, were Vanessa and Haley. Vanessa looked as if she were recovering nicely, I noted. The only indication that she'd hit her head was a small Elastoplast over a yellow-blue fading bruised spot on her forehead near the hairline. I caught Mal's eye and winked slightly. Then we stepped inside.

"Hi," said Danielle. Mal and I said hello, but Becca, Charlotte, Vanessa and Haley pointedly refused even to look in Danielle's direction.

"This way, please," said Stacey, leading the way to the playroom. She sat down in an armchair and Danielle sat on a cushion in front of it. Mal and Jessi sat on the sofa. The other four conspicuously sat as far away from Danielle as possible. It would have been funny if Danielle's face hadn't been so woebegone.

"Now," said Stacey, "we're going to talk."

Vanessa said, "I have nothing to say."

Mal gave her sister a poke. "What, did the accident do something to your tongue?"

Vanessa turned and stuck her tongue out at her sister and I hid a grin. Mal rolled her eyes.

"Okay, let me ask you this," began Stacey. "Suppose someone said, 'Get into this train. I'm going to drive it off the Brooklyn Bridge.' Would you do it?"

The four girls exchanged glances. Then Becca said, "Of course not. That would be stupid!"

"So you'd think for yourself and say no," said Stacey.

Becca frowned. "Yes."

"You'd be able to work that out?" Stacey continued. "So if someone told you that you had to get on that train, what would you do?"

"I wouldn't get on," said Vanessa grudgingly. She could see where Stacey was leading.

"So if you were able to work out that getting on that train wasn't such a great idea, and then you did it anyway, wouldn't you be at least partially responsible?"

"She *said* she knew how to drive the car!" Haley burst out. "And *I* got into trouble!"

"But I'm sorry. I didn't mean for the car to crash! I didn't mean for you to get hurt, Vanessa. I wouldn't hurt any of you for *anything*!" Danielle cried.

"You could have killed us!" Vanessa bounced to her feet and pointed dramatically at the little Elastoplast on her forehead. "And you got us all into big trouble! Huge. Enormous! Elephantic!"

"Elephantic?" Mal couldn't help but ask. Vanessa wants to be a poet and she often comes up with words that, well, might not exactly be real words.

"Big," said Vanessa impatiently. "Like an elephant."

I put my hand up quickly to cover the smile I couldn't quite stop. I felt terrible for Danielle. But Vanessa's dramatics *were* funny.

Mal caught my eye, then looked quickly down at the toes of her snowboots.

Stacey said, "Okay. So you're right. You all got into trouble. And it's Danielle's fault. You win. She's wrong, you're right. What do you gain by never speaking to her again?"

A small silence fell over the room. Then Becca said, in a soft voice, "I'm *not*. I mean, I'm *not* ever going to speak to Danielle again."

"Don't tell *me* about it," said Stacey folding her arms. "I know how important my friends are. And how I count on them. And how I need them. I also know that part of friendship is forgiving people— and accepting things about them that you can't change."

I was impressed. The atmosphere in the room had been outright hostile when we'd started talking. But Stacey had given the girls something to think about. And I could see that they were starting to make eye contact again.

Haley smiled. "You're my buddy,

Danielle," she said. "Even if you are a kangaroo!"

"A kangaroo!" said Danielle.

"Ideas just hop out of your head." Haley shrugged. "I suppose it's hard not to just hop along with them."

Smiles began to show on the girls' faces. Then Danielle said quietly, "I am sorry. I'm really sorry. I'll never, ever do something like that again."

"Never is a long time," said Stacey. "How about if you just try to think through what you're doing?"

"Yes," said Haley. "Look before you leap."

"Like a kangaroo, that's what you do," said Vanessa. She was speaking in rhyme, which she does when she's feeling good. Things were going to be all right.

"Hey, what about my snack?" Greg was standing in the doorway.

"I could do with some hot chocolate," said Mal. "What about you lot?"

"Cool!" said Becca.

"No, silly, hot!" said Vanessa. Everyone burst into giggles and we all went into the kitchen.

The fight was over.

I looked at Mal and raised my own cup of hot chocolate. I knew we were thinking the same thing.

123

Not only was the fight over, but in my eyes, Stacey was back. Her recent odd behaviour had been annoying. But like Stacey said, friends have to forgive—and accept—if they want to stay friends.

"Hey, Stace!" I said.

Stacey looked at Mal and me.

"Good work," I said softly.

# 14th CHAPTER

So the fight was over.

Which left me with just one little problem.

The wedding that wasn't. I just hadn't been able to admit that Aunt Cecelia hadn't got married. Danielle's short driving career had kept everyone's attention for a while, but now I had to duck all kinds of questions.

Sooner or later I was going to have to admit that I'd made a big mistake. A major goof. And I was going to feel like a world-class dope when I did.

No way out of it. Unless . . .

The idea came to me at precisely 5:42 A.M. while I was practising at the *barre* in our basement. I stopped in mid-*plié* and stared at my reflection in the mirror, my mouth open.

Unless there *was* a wedding. If Becca and I could persuade Aunt Cecelia and Mr Major to fall in love and get married after all, I might not ever have to confess my foolish mistake.

And what could be easier? I mean, Mr Major was super-nice. (I'd seen him once since the wedding and he hadn't even mentioned Becca's and my monumental goof. Instead, he'd congratulated me on "keeping a cool head in an emergency".) And he was handsome. And Aunt Cecelia already liked him or she wouldn't be spending time with him. So why not just give their romance (by then I'd convinced myself that a romance was already in the works) a little push in the right direction?

I could hardly wait to put my plan into action.

"You think so?" asked Becca, when I told her. "You think they might really be in love and not know it?"

"That's it." I nodded. "They just need our help. You know, the way Dawn's mum and Mary Anne's dad needed a little help in getting together."

"Wow!" said Becca. "What shall we do?"

"A romantic dinner, just for two," I said. "Candlelight, flowers, soft music, you know. Like at a smart restaurant, like Chez Maurice."

Becca looked unhappy. "But Jessi, we can't afford to pay for dinner for Aunt Cecelia and Mr Major at Chez Maurice. Can we?"

"No, of course not. But we can plan a special dinner for them right here. One that is just as good. And just as romantic."

"Will Mama and Daddy let us do that?" asked Becca.

"We'll do it when they're going to be out for the evening. You know Aunt Cecelia usually stays around when they go out, even though I'm old enough to be left alone with you and Squirt."

So we put plan Get Aunt Cecelia Married into action. I rang Mr Major and invited him over for the very next evening that Mama and Daddy were going out. "We were wondering if you could call in," I said.

"Is there a problem?" asked Mr Major. He sounded puzzled.

"Er, it's nothing much. I mean, I can explain it better when you get here," I hurried on.

"Well, okay," he said.

"Great! We'll look forward to seeing you. Aunt Cecelia too," I added.

I heard Mr Major laughing as I rang

off. What had I said that was so funny? I wondered. But I didn't have much time to think about it. We had a romantic evening to plan.

Over the next couple of days, Becca and I got candles, and the ingredients for a romantic dinner. Well, anyway, for spaghetti. Becca thought it was romantic because it was the same meal that the two dogs shared in *Lady and the Tramp*. I wasn't sure garlic was the most romantic ingredient in a meal, but if they both ate some then it wouldn't be a problem, right?

The night Mr Major was supposed to come, I was terrified that Mama or Daddy (or both of them) would come home from work instead of going straight out for an early dinner before the performance of the Stoneybrook Chamber Music Ensemble. But they didn't.

Becca and I had planned everything very carefully. And we'd coordinated our watches. Exactly fifty minutes before Mr Major was scheduled to arrive, Becca got things started.

"Aunt Cecelia! Aunt Cecelia!" she called from her room.

"What is it, Becca?"

"Could you come here and help me with my maths? I've got a test tomorrow. It's really important."

"Certainly."

"Go ahead," I said to my aunt. "I'll start dinner and put Squirt to bed."

"Well ... what about your homework?"

"All done. Go ahead."

"Okay." Aunt Cecelia untied her apron and left the kitchen.

Quickly I put aside the leftover meatloaf she'd just taken out to reheat and started the spaghetti. Then I laid the dining room table and put the flowers Becca and I had bought that afternoon in the centre of the table in our best vase. Last of all, I turned the overhead light down *low* and lit the candles.

The doorbell rang. I surveyed the dining room. Perfect. It couldn't be more romantic, not even at Chez Maurice.

Aunt Cecelia and Mr Major just had to fall in love.

"I'll get it," I called.

A moment later I ushered Mr Major into the dining room—just as Becca led Aunt Cecelia in.

The two of them stopped. Becca and I watched them closely. Were they exchanging a meaningful glance? Realizing that it was always meant to be? Casting caution and reserve to the winds?

No, they were not.

They were smiling. And then they were laughing.

Becca put her hands on her hips. "What's so funny?"

"Nothing. I mean, well, it's a lovely dinner, girls," said Aunt Cecelia. "But I'm afraid that Mr Major and I have something to tell you. We really don't want to get married. We're friends. Good friends."

"Have been for a long time," said Mr Major. "We met on a blind date, as a matter of fact. Remember that, Cece?"

Aunt Cecelia laughed. "Do I ever! The worst blind date I was ever on!"

"Me, too," said Mr Major. "But I made one of the best friends I've had."

"Are you sure?" I couldn't help but ask.

"Positive," said Aunt Cecelia. "But thanks for all your work."

"And now I'd like to invite you to join us at this lovely dinner," said Mr Major.

Becca and I looked at each other. What could we do? A wedding between Aunt Cecelia and Mr Major just wasn't going to happen.

I sighed. Then Becca and I got out extra plates and cutlery.

And you know what? It was pretty good spaghetti in spite of everything.

# 15th
# CHAPTER

The meeting of the Babysitters Club had just come to order. We were all there, including Logan, and we were all on time.

And we were all laughing.

"So you ate a *romantic* spaghetti dinner—just the four of you! I can't believe it!" cried Claudia.

"What's wrong with spaghetti?" asked Logan.

"It's great," said Stacey. "It's just sort of messy for a romantic dinner."

"I think it was a great idea," said Mary Anne. "It could have worked."

You've guessed it. I had just told them about the wedding that wasn't. "I hope you lot didn't buy a present," I said.

Stacey said, "Well, we'd budgeted for one. I think we'd better spend it on something important. Like a pizza party."

"Good idea," said Kristy. "In fact, that's an excellent idea."

"And don't think we're going to let you live this down," said Mallory. "You haven't heard the last of it, Jessi Ramsey!"

"I can take it," I said. "Just wait. Your turn will come."

Mary Anne said, "Well, I think Aunt Cecelia's getting married would be terrific. And it might happen. Never say never."

"Never will," I agreed. I shot a sly look at Stacey. "Just like Stacey taught Vanessa and Charlotte and Haley and Becca."

"Here's to Stacey!" said Claudia, raising a coconut cream puff in salute.

Stacey looked pleased. "I'm glad I could help," she said. "It would have been terrible for those kids to stop being friends over one of Danielle's crazy ideas."

"And like you said, they went along with it, even though they *knew* that something like driving a car was a big-time bad idea," I reminded her.

"Not to mention tobogganing in the basement," said Dawn.

"And making the bathroom into a swimming pool," said Kristy. She snorted. "But you know, it wasn't such a bad idea really. I mean, it kind of made sense, if you thought about it. . ."

We all started laughing at that.

"Maybe Danielle will grow up to be like you, Kristy," Mary Anne teased gently. "An ideas person."

"And chairman of a fine organization like the BSC," said Logan.

It was good to be there with my friends. I hoped Danielle and her friends really were all friends again.

The sound of the doorbell interrupted our thoughts.

"Hey, have we ordered pizza already?" asked Claudia in mock surprise.

"Not yet, Claud. But we will soon," promised Stacey.

Claudia jumped up and ran to answer the door.

A few moments later we heard her call, "Hey, you lot, come here!"

"In the middle of a meeting?" Kristy called back.

"Yes!"

"Is it an emergency?"

"*Kristy!*" shrieked Claudia.

"Okay, okay. This meeting of the BSC is adjourned four minutes early today," said Kristy. "And this had better be good."

We trooped to the front door. Claudia

stepped back and flung it wide open.

Five very strangely costumed creatures stood there: someone in a long doctor's coat with a stethoscope and big weird glasses. Someone in a witch's hat and costume. A police officer. A cat. And a ghost.

"Trick or treat!" five voices shouted.

"Trick or treat!" said Kristy. "What?"

"We're playing Hallowe'en," explained the doctor. It was, of course, Danielle.

"It was Danielle's idea," said Becca. "Isn't it a great one?"

"It is," said Claudia.

"Really," Stacey said.

"I wish I'd thought of it," said Kristy.

"So trick or treat," said Danielle, holding out a paper bag.

"Whoa! Wait here," said Claudia. She ran upstairs, followed by Stacey.

I looked at the grinning assortment of creatures on the steps and knew that Danielle and her friends were really over their fight. And that whatever had happened hadn't daunted Danielle's imagination.

Who knew what she was capable of? I looked forward to her future. And I knew I was lucky to be a part of her present.

Then Claudia reappeared with Stacey. Their arms were heaped with junk food.

"Treat!" said Claudia. "Here, everybody, help us."

So the members of the BSC helped. We took packets of Jaffa Cakes and of Gummi Worms and Sweethearts and all kinds of sweets and junk food that Claudia had hidden around her room, and we gave them to the trick-or-treaters.

"Happy Un-Hallowe'en!" we called as they turned to go.

"And many more," I said softly, watching Danielle lead the way.

Look out for No 83

## STACEY VERSUS THE BSC

I had *vowed* to be at this meeting on time.
After what happened Friday, I knew I'd
be in trouble. Dawn had had a whole
weekend to tell everybody the news.

I needed wings. Better yet, a time
warp.

My bad deeds were piling up. A few
latenesses, a few skipped jobs . . . I could
already hear Kristy's lecture.

*Lecture?* Iron shackles, maybe.

Robert and I raced down Elm Street
and up Bradford Court. We said a quick
goodbye in front of the Kishis' house. I
barged inside, ran upstairs, and hurried
through Claudia's bedroom door.

Facing me were the Six Sisters of
Doom: Grim, Grumpy, Glum, Sullen
Sombre and Bleak.

"Hi," I said with my friendliest smile.

Shift, hrrmph, grumble, cough, was the response.

"Sorry I'm late," I continued. "See, my mum was installing this exercise machine—"

Kristy cleared her throat. "It isn't just *this* lateness, Stacey."

"Oh?" I must have been nervous. My voice sounded like Tweetie Bird's.

"You've been on another planet lately," Kristy continued. "I mean, do you want to be in the club?"

"Of course I do!" I replied.

"Well, you don't *act* like it. It's bad enough that you're breaking rules about subbing—"

"Kristy, I'm sorry—"

"But you *tricked* Mary Anne," Kristy barged on. "I think you owe her an apology."

Mary Anne was looking at the bedspread. Her hair was falling in front of her face. "No, it's all right," she said.

I could tell it wasn't.